St. Nicholas:
The Believer

*A New Story For Christmas
Based On The Old Story
Of St. Nicholas*

Eric & Lana Elder

*To Angie,
So nice to meet
you today! And what
a wonderful heart you
have for serving +
blessing others!
The Lord sees
and will
reward you!
(Hebrews 11:6)
Eric Elder
12/1/2018*

St. Nicholas: The Believer
Copyright © 2009-2014 Eric & Lana Elder.
All rights reserved.

St. Nicholas: The Believer is one of
several inspirational resources produced by
Eric Elder Ministries. For more inspiring
books and music, please visit:
WWW.INSPIRINGBOOKS.COM

ISBN 978-1-931760-40-9

DEDICATION

*This book is dedicated to my sweet wife,
Lana, who inspired me and helped me to
tell you this spectacular story.*

*Lana had just finished making her final
edits and suggestions on this book the week
before she passed from this life to the next,
way too young at the age of 48.*

*It was her idea and her dream to share the
story of St. Nicholas with as many people
as possible. She wanted to inspire them to
give their lives to others as Jesus had given
His life for us. This book is the first step
in making that dream a reality.*

*To the world Lana may have been just
one person, but to me she was the world.
This book is lovingly dedicated to her.*

INTRODUCTION
by Eric Elder

There was a time when I almost gave up celebrating Christmas. Our kids were still young and weren't yet hooked on the idea of Santa Claus and presents, Christmas trees and decorations.

I had read that the Puritans who first came to America were so zealous in their faith that they didn't celebrate Christmas at all. Instead they charged fines to businesses in their community who failed to keep their shops *open* on Christmas day. They didn't want anything to do with a holiday that was, they felt, rooted in paganism. As a new believer and a new father myself, the idea of going against the flow of the excesses of Christmas had its appeal, at least in some respects.

Then I read an article by a man who simply loved celebrating Christmas. He could think of no greater way to celebrate the birth of the most important figure in human history than throwing the grandest of parties for Him—gathering and feasting and sharing gifts with as many of his family and friends as possible. This man was a pastor of deep faith and great joy. For him, the joy of Christ's birth was so wondrous that he reveled in every aspect of Christmas, including all the planning, decorating and activities that went along with it. He even loved bringing Santa Claus into the festivities, our modern-day version of the very real and very ancient Saint Nicholas, a man of deep faith and great joy as well who Himself worshipped and adored the Baby who was born in Bethlehem.

So why *not* celebrate the birth of Christ? Why *not* make it the biggest party of the year? Why *not* make it the "Hap-Happiest season of all"?

I was sold. Christmas could stay—and my kids would be much hap-happier for it, too.

I dove back into celebrating Christmas with full vigor, and at the same time took a closer look into the life of the real Saint Nicholas, a man who seemed almost irremovably intertwined with this Holy Day. I discovered that Saint Nicholas and Santa Claus were indeed one and the same, and that the Saint Nicholas who lived in the 3rd and 4th centuries after the birth of Christ was truly a devout follower of Christ himself.

As my wife and I read more and more about Nicholas' fascinating story, we became enthralled with this believer who had already been capturing the hearts and imaginations of believers and nonbelievers alike throughout the centuries.

With so many books and movies that go to great lengths to tell you the "true" story of Santa Claus (and how his reindeer are really powered by everything from egg nog to Coca-Cola), I've found that there are very few stories that even come close to describing the actual person of who Saint Nicholas was, and in particular, what he thought about the Man for whom Christmas is named, Jesus Christ. I was surprised to learn that with all the historical documents that attest to Saint Nicholas' faith in Christ, compelling tellings of those stories seem to have fallen by the wayside over the ages.

So with the encouragement and help of my sweet wife, Lana, we decided to bring the story of Saint Nicholas back to life for you, with a desire to help you recapture the essence of Christmas for yourself.

While some people, with good reason, may still go to great lengths to try to remove anything that might possibly hint of secularism from this holiest day of the year, it seems to me equally fitting to go to great lengths to try to restore Santa to his rightful place—not as the patron saint of shopping malls, but as a beacon of light that shines brightly on the One for whom this Holy Day is named.

It is with deep faith and great joy that I offer you this Christmas novella—a little story. I've enjoyed telling it and I hope you'll enjoy hearing it. It just may be the most human telling of the story of Saint Nicholas you've ever heard.

Above all, I pray that God will use this story to rekindle your love, not only for this season of the year, but for the One who makes this season so bright.

May God bless you this Christmas and always!

In Christ's love,
Eric Elder

P.S. I've divided this story into 7 parts and 40 chapters to make it easier to read. If you'd like, you can read a part a day for 7 days leading up to Christmas. Or if you'd like to use this book as a daily devotional, you can read a chapter a day for 40 days leading up to Christmas, counting the Prologue, Epilogue and Conclusion as separate chapters. If you start on November 15th, you'll finish on Christmas Eve!

PART 1

PROLOGUE

My name is Dimitri—Dimitri Alexander. But that's not important. What's important is that man over there, lying on his bed. He's—well, I suppose there's really no better way to describe him except to say—he's a saint. Not just because of all the good he's done, but because he was—as a saint always is—a *Believer*. He believed that there was Someone in life who was greater than he was, Someone who guided him, who helped him through every one of his days.

If you were to look at him closely, lying there on his bed, it might look to you as if he was dead. And in some sense, I guess you would be right. But the truth is, he's more alive now than he has ever been.

My friends and I have come here today to spend his last day on earth with him. Just a few minutes ago we watched as he passed from this life to the next.

I should be crying, I know. Believe me, I have been—and I will be again. But for now, I can't help but simply be grateful that he has finally made it to his new home, a home that he has been dreaming about for many years. A home where he can finally talk to God face to face, like I'm talking to you right now.

Oh, he was a saint all right. But to me, and to so many others, he was something even more. He was—how could I put it? An inspiration. A friend. A teacher. A helper. A giver. Oh, he loved to give and give and give some more, until it seemed he had nothing left to give at all. But then he'd reach down deep and find a little more. "There's always *something* you can give," as he would often say.

He always hoped, in some small way, that he could use his life to make a difference in the world. He wanted, above all, to help people. But with so many needs all around, what could he possibly do?

He was like a man on a beach surrounded by starfish that had been washed up onto the shore. He knew that they would die if they didn't make it back into the water.

Not knowing how to save them all, the man on the beach did what he could. He reached down, picked one up, and tossed it back into the water. Then reached down again, picked up another, and did the same.

Someone once asked the man why he bothered at all—that with so many needs all around, how could he possibly make any difference. He'd just toss another starfish into the water and say, "It made a difference to that one." Then he'd reach down and pick up another.

You see, to the world you may be just one person, but to one person you may be the world.

In many ways, my friend was just like you and me. Each one of us has just one life to live. But if you live it right, one life is all you need. And if you live your life for God, well, you just might touch the whole world.

Did his life make any difference? I already know my answer, because I'm one of those that he reached down and picked up many, many years ago. But how about I tell you his story, and when I get to the end, I'll let you decide if his life made a difference or not. And then maybe, by the time we're finished, you'll see that *your* life can make a difference, too.

Oh, by the way, I haven't told you his name yet, this man who was such a great saint, such a great believer in the God who loved him, who created him, who sustained him and with whom he is now living forever.

His name is Nicholas—and this is his story.

CHAPTER 1

Nicholas lived in an ideal world. At least that's the way he saw it. As a nine-year-old boy, growing up on the northern coast of what he called the Great Sea—you might call it the Mediterranean—Nicholas couldn't imagine a better life.

He would often walk through the streets with his father, acting as if they were on their way to somewhere in particular. But the real reason for their outing was to look for someone who was struggling to make ends meet, someone who needed a lift in their life. A simple hello often turned into the discovery of a need to be met. Nicholas and his father would pray, and if they could meet the need, they found a way to do it.

Nicholas couldn't count the number of times his dad would sneak up behind someone afterwards and put some apples in their sack, or a small coin or two. As far as Nicholas knew, no one ever knew what his father had done, except to say that sometimes they heard people talking about the miracle of receiving exactly what they needed at just the right time, in some unexpected way.

Nicholas loved these walks with his father, just as he loved his time at home with his mother. They had shown the same love and generosity with him as they had shown to so many others.

His parents had somehow found a way to prosper, even in the turbulent times in which they lived. They were, in fact, quite wealthy. But whether their family was rich or poor seemed to make no difference to Nicholas. All he knew or cared about was that his parents loved him like no one else on earth. He was their only son, and their times together were simple and truly joyful.

Their richest times came at night, as they shared stories with each other that they had heard about a Man who was like no other Man they had ever known. A Man who lived on the other side of the Great Sea about 280 years earlier. His name was Jesus. Nicholas was enthralled with the stories of this Man who seemed to be so precious in the eyes of his parents. Jesus seemed both down-to-earth and larger-than-life, all at the same time. How could anyone be so humble, yet so noble? How could He be so poor that He was born in an animal stable, yet so generous that He could feed 5,000 people? How could He live His life so fully, yet die a death so cruelly? Jesus was, to Nicholas, an enigma, the most fascinating person about whom he'd ever heard. One day, Nicholas thought to himself, he hoped to visit this land on the other side of the sea—and walk where Jesus walked.

For all the love that Nicholas and his parents shared and which held them together, there was one thing that threatened to pull them apart. It was the one thing that seemed to be threatening many families in their country these days, irrespective of their wealth or poverty, their faith or lack of faith, their love for others or their lack of love.

Nicholas' friends and neighbors called it *the plague*. His parents had mentioned it from time to time, but only in their prayers. They prayed for the families who were affected by the plague, asking God for healing when possible, and for strength of faith when not. Most of all, his parents prayed for Nicholas that regardless of what happened around him, he would always know how very much they loved him, and how very much God loved him.

Even though Nicholas was so young, he had seen enough of life to know that real threats existed in the world. Yet he also had been shielded from those threats, in a way, by the love of his parents and by their devout faith in God. As his father had learned over the years, and had many times reminded Nicholas, "In *all* things, God works for the good of those who love Him." And Nicholas believed him. Up to this point, he'd had no real reason to doubt the words his father had spoken.

But it would be only a matter of months before Nicholas' faith would be challenged and he would have to decide if he really believed those words for himself—that in *all* things, God would truly work for the good of those who loved Him.

Tonight, however, he simply trusted the words of his father, listening to his parents' prayers for him—and for those in his city—as he drifted off into a perfect sleep.

CHAPTER 2

Nicholas woke to the sounds of birds out his window. The air was fresh, washed clean by the seaside mist in the early morning.

But the news this morning was less than idyllic. A friend of Nicholas' family had contracted the sickness that they had only heard about from people in other cities. The boy was said to be near the point of death.

Nicholas' father had heard the news first and had gone to pray for the boy. Returning home just as Nicholas awoke, his father shared the news with his wife and with Nicholas.

"We need to pray," he said, with no hint of panic in his voice, but with an unmistakable urgency that caused all three of them to slip down to their knees.

Nicholas' father began the prayer: "Father, You know the plans You have for this child.

We trust You to carry them out. We pray for Your healing as we love this boy, but we know that You love him even more than we do. We trust that as we place him in Your hands this morning, You will work *all* things together for good, as You always do for those who love You."

It was a prayer Nicholas had heard his father pray many times before, asking for what they believed was best in every situation, but trusting that God knew best in the end. It was the same type of prayer Nicholas had heard that Jesus had prayed the night before He died: "If You are willing," Jesus prayed, "take this cup from Me. Yet not My will, but Yours be done."

Nicholas never quite knew what to make of this prayer. Wouldn't God always want what's best for us? And how could someone's death ever be a good thing? Yet his father prayed that prayer so often, and with such sincerity of heart, that Nicholas was confident that it was the right thing to pray. But how God could answer any other way than healing the boy—and still work it out for good—remained a mystery.

After Nicholas' mother had added her own

words to the prayer, and Nicholas himself had joined in, his father concluded with thanks to God for listening—and for already answering their prayers.

As they stood, the news came to their door, as if in direct answer to what they had just prayed. But it wasn't the answer they were hoping for. The boy had died.

Nicholas' mother began to weep quietly, but not holding back on her tears. She wept as she felt the loss of another mother, feeling the loss as if it were her own son who had died.

Nicholas' father took hold of her hand and pulled Nicholas close, saying a quiet prayer for the family of the boy who had died, and adding another prayer for his own family. He gave his wife and son one more final squeeze, then walked out the door to return to the other boy's home.

CHAPTER 3

The boy's death had a sobering effect on the whole city. The people had known the boy, of course, and were sad for the family.

But his death was more sobering because it wasn't an isolated event. The people had heard stories of how the sickness had been spreading through the cities around them, taking the lives of not just one or two people here and there, but entire families—entire neighborhoods. The death of this boy seemed to indicate that the plague had now arrived in their city, too.

No one knew how to stop it. All they could do was pray. And pray they did.

As the sickness began to spread, Nicholas' parents would visit the homes of those who lay dying. While his parents' money was powerless to offer relief to the families, their prayers brought a peace that no amount of money could buy.

As always, Nicholas' father would pray that death would pass them over, as it had passed over the Israelites in Egypt when the plague of death overtook the lives of the firstborn of every family that wasn't willing to honor God. But this sickness was different. It made no distinction between believer or unbeliever, firstborn or last born, or any other apparent factor. This sickness seemed to know no bounds, and seemed unstoppable by any means.

Yet Nicholas watched as his father prayed in faith nonetheless, believing that God could stop the plague at any moment, at any household, and trusting God to work it all out for good, even if their lives, too, were seemingly cut short.

These latter prayers were what people clung to the most. More than anything else, these words gave them hope—hope that their lives were not lived in vain, hope that their deaths were not going unnoticed by the God who created them.

A visit by Nicholas' father and mother spoke volumes to those who were facing unbearable pain, for as the plague spread, fewer and fewer people had been willing to leave their own homes, let alone visit the homes where the sickness had struck. The prayers of Nicholas' father, and the tears of his mother, gave the families the strength they needed to face whatever came their way.

Nicholas watched in wonder as his parents dispensed their gifts of mercy during the day, then returned home each night physically spent, but spiritually strengthened. It made him wonder how they got their strength for each day. But it also made him wonder how long their own family could remain untouched by this plague.

When Nicholas finally found the courage to voice this question out loud, a question that seemed to be close to all of their hearts, his father simply answered that they had only two choices: to live in fear, or to live in love, and to follow the example of the One in whom they had entrusted their lives. They chose to live in love, doing for others what they would want others to do for them.

So every morning Nicholas' father and mother would wake up and pray, asking their Lord what He would have them do. Then, pushing aside any fears they might have had, they put their trust in God, spending the day serving others as if they were serving Christ Himself.

While his father's response didn't answer the immediate question on Nicholas' heart—which was how much longer it might be till the sickness visited their own home—it seemed to answer a question that went much deeper. It answered the question of whether or not God was aware of all that was going on, and if He was, whether or not He cared enough to do anything about it.

By the way that God seemed to be directing his parents each day, Nicholas gained a peace of mind that God was indeed fully aware of all that was going on in the lives of every person in his city of Patara—and that God did indeed care. God cared enough to send Nicholas' parents to those who needed to hear a word from Him, who needed a touch from His hands, who needed a touch from God not just in their flesh, but in their spirits as well.

It seemed to Nicholas to be a more glorious answer to his question than he could have imagined. His worry about when the sickness might visit their own home dissipated as he went to sleep that night. Instead, he prayed that God would use his own hands and words —Nicholas' hands and words—as if they were God's very own, reaching out to express God's love for His people.

CHAPTER 4

In the coming days, Nicholas found himself wanting to help his father and mother more and more as they delivered God's mercy to those around them.

They worked together to bring food, comfort and love to each family touched by the plague. Some days it was as simple as stopping by to let a mother know she wasn't alone. Others days it was bringing food or drink to an entire family who had taken ill. And still other days it was preparing a place in the hills around their city where they carefully laid the bodies of those who had succumbed to the sickness and whose spirits had passed from this life to the next.

Each day Nicholas' heart grew more and more aware of the temporal nature of life on earth, and more and more in tune with the eternal nature of the life that is unseen. It seemed to Nicholas that the line between the two worlds was becoming less and less distinct. What he had once thought of as solid and real—like rocks and trees, or hands and feet—soon took on a more ethereal nature. And those things that were more difficult for him to touch before—like faith and hope, love and peace—began to become more solid and real.

It was as if his world was turning both upside down and inside out at the same time, not with a gut-wrenching twisting, but as if his eyes themselves were being re-calibrated, adjusting better to see with more clarity what was really going on—focusing more acutely on what really mattered in life. Even surrounded by so much sickness and death, Nicholas felt himself coming alive more fully than he'd ever felt before.

His father tried to describe what Nicholas was feeling by using words that he'd heard Jesus had said, that whoever tried to hold onto this life too tightly would lose it, but whoever was willing to let go of this life, would find true life. By learning how to love others without being constrained by fear, being propelled forward by love instead, Nicholas was starting to experience how it felt to truly live.

Whether that feeling could sustain him through what lay ahead, he didn't know. But what he did know was that for now, more than anything else, he wanted to live each day to the fullest. He wanted to wake up each day looking for how God could use him, then do whatever God was willing to give him to do. To do anything less would be to shortchange himself from living the life God had given him to live—and to shortchange God from the work God wanted to get done.

As the days passed, Nicholas came to know what his father and mother already knew: that no one knew how many more days they had left in this world. His family no longer saw themselves as human beings having a temporary spiritual experience, but as spiritual beings, having a temporary human experience. With eyes of faith, they were able to look into whatever lay ahead of them without the fear that gripped so many of the others around them.

CHAPTER 5

When Nicholas awoke one day to the sound of his mother coughing, time seemed to stand still.

For all the preparation his parents—and his own faith—had given him, it still caught him off guard to think that the sickness might have finally crossed over the threshold of their own home.

He thought that maybe God would spare them for all the kindness they had shown to others during the previous few months. But his father had cautioned him against such thinking, reminding him that for all the good that Jesus had done in His life—for all the healing that He had brought to others—there still came a time when He, too, had to face suffering and death. It didn't mean that God didn't love Jesus, or wasn't concerned for Him, or hadn't seen all the good He had done in His life. And it didn't mean that Jesus remained indifferent to what was about to take place either. Jesus even told His disciples that His heart was deeply troubled by what He was about to go through, but that didn't mean He shrank back from what lay ahead of Him. No, He said, it was for this very hour that He had come. Greater love, He told His disciples, had no one than this: that they lay down their lives for their friends.

Nicholas' mother coughed again, and time slowly began to move again for Nicholas. He stood to his feet. As he approached his mother, she hesitated for a moment. It was as if she was torn between wanting him to stand still—not to come one step closer to the sickness that had now reached her body—or to get up on her feet, too, and throw her arms around him, assuring him that everything would be all right. But a moment later, Nicholas had made her decision unnecessary, for he was already in her arms, holding on as tight as he could as they both broke down in tears. As Nicholas was learning, having faith doesn't mean you can't cry. It just means that you can trust God, even with your tears.

Nicholas' father had already shed some of his own tears that morning. He had gone outside before the sunrise, this time not to visit the homes of others, but to pray. For him, the place where he always returned when he needed to be alone with God was to the fresh air by the sea, not far from their home. While he knew he could pray anywhere, at any time, it was by the sea that he felt closest to God. The sound of the waves, rhythmically washing up on the shore, seemed to have a calming, mesmerizing effect on him.

He had arrived in time to watch the sunrise off to his left, looking down the shoreline of the Great Sea. How many sunrises had he seen from that very spot? And how many more would he have left to see? He turned his head and coughed, letting the question roll back out to sea with the next receding wave. The sickness had come upon him as well.

This wasn't the first time he had asked himself how many days he had left to live. The difference this time was that in the past, he had always asked it hypothetically. He would come to this spot whenever he had an important decision to make, a decision that required he think beyond the short term. He would come here when he needed to look into eternity, taking into account the brevity of life. Here, at the edge of the sea, it was as if he could grasp both the brevity of life and the eternity of heaven at the same time.

The daily rising of the sun and the swelling, cresting and breaking of the waves on the shore reminded him that God was still in control, that His world would carry on—with or without him—just as it had since God had first spoken the water and earth into existence, and just as it would until the day God would choose for its end, to make way for the new heaven and the new earth. In light of eternity, the lifespan of the earth seemed incredibly short, and the lifespan of man even shorter still. In that short span of life, he knew that he had to make the most of each day, not just living for himself, and not even just living for others, but ultimately living for the God who had given him life. If God, the Creator of all things, had seen fit to breathe into him the breath of life, then as long as he could still take a breath, he wanted to make the most of it.

Coughing again, Nicholas' father remembered that this was no mere intellectual exercise to help him come to grips with a difficult decision. This time—as he looked out at the sunrise once more, and at one more wave rolling in—he realized that this was the final test of everything that he had believed up until this point.

Some of life's tests he had passed with flying colors. Others he had failed when fear or doubt had taken over. But this was a test he knew he wanted to pass more than any other.

He closed his eyes and asked for strength for another day. He let the sun warm his face, and he gently opened the palms of his hands to feel the breeze as it lifted up along the shore and floated over his body. He opened his eyes and looked one more time at the sea.

Then he turned and walked toward home, where he would soon join his precious wife and his beloved son in a long, tearful embrace.

PART 2

CHAPTER 6

Nicholas stood alone. He was on the same stretch of beach where his father had stood just ten years earlier, looking out at the sunrise and the waves on the seashore.

Nicholas' father never made it out to look at the Great Sea again, having finally succumbed to the sickness himself. Nicholas' mother passed away first, within two weeks of the first signs of illness. His father lasted another three days after that, as if holding on as long as he could to make sure his wife passed as peacefully as possible from this life to the next, and making sure Nicholas was as ready as possible to take the next steps in his own life.

Nicholas' father didn't shy away from tears, but he didn't want them wasted on wrongful emotions either. "Don't cry because it's over," his father had said to both his wife and his son. "Smile because it was beautiful."

There was a time and place for anger and disappointment, but this wasn't the time for either. If given the chance to do it all over again, his parents would have chosen to do exactly what they did. It was not foolishness, they said, to be willing to risk their lives for the sake of others, especially when there were no guarantees that they would have survived anyway.

As it turned out, the plague ended up taking the lives of almost a third of the people in Patara before it finally ran its course. The sickness seemed to have a mind of its own, affecting those who tried to shield themselves from it as well as those who, like his parents, had ventured out into the midst of it.

After the death of his parents, Nicholas felt a renewed sense of urgency to pick up where they had left off, visiting those who were sick and comforting the families of those who had died.

Then, almost as suddenly as it came to their city, the plague left. Nicholas had spent most of the next few weeks sleeping, trying to recover from the long days—and even longer nights—of ministering to those who were affected. When he was awake, he spent his time trying to process his own feelings and emotions in light of the loss of the family he loved. In so many ways, his parents *were* his life. His life was so intertwined with theirs, and having them taken so suddenly from him, he hardly knew what to do without them. He went to live with his uncle, a priest who lived in the monastery in Patara, until he was ready to venture out further into the world on his own. Now that time had come, and it was time for Nicholas to make his decision.

Unlike many others who had been orphaned by the plague, Nicholas had been left with a sizable inheritance. The question on his heart wasn't what he would do to make a living, but what he would do to make a life. Through all that he had experienced, and now recognizing the brevity of life for himself, Nicholas now knew why his father had come so often to this shore to pray. Now it was Nicholas' turn to consider his own future in light of eternity.

What should I do? Where should I go? How should I spend the rest of my days? The questions could have overwhelmed him, except that his father had prepared him well for moments like these, too.

His father, always a student of the writings of Scripture and of the life of Christ, had told him that Jesus taught that we needn't worry so much about the trouble down the road as just the trouble for that day. Each day has enough trouble of its own, Jesus said.

As Nicholas thought about this, his burden lifted. He didn't have to figure out what he was going to do with the rest of his life just yet. He only had to decide on his next step.

He had enough money to travel the length of the entire world back and forth three times and still have enough to live on for years to come. But that wasn't really what he wanted to do. He had never had a desire to live wildly or lavishly, for the life he knew up to this point already gave him tremendous satisfaction. But there *was* one place he had always wanted to see with his own eyes.

As he looked out across the sea, to the south and to the west, he knew that somewhere in between lay the place he most wanted to visit—a land that seemed more precious in his mind than any other. It was the land where Jesus had lived, the land where He had walked and taught, the land where He was born and died, and the land where so many of the stories of His life—and almost the entirety of Scripture itself—had taken place.

Nicholas knew that some decisions in life were made only through the sweat and agony of prayer, trying desperately to decide between two seemingly good, but mutually exclusive paths. But this decision was not one of them. This was one of those decisions that, by the nature of the circumstances, was utterly simple to make. Apart from his uncle, there was little more to keep him in Patara, and nothing to stop him from following the desire that had been on his heart for so long.

He was glad his father had shown him this spot, and he was glad that he had come to it again today. He knew exactly what he was going to do next. His decision was as clear as the water in front of him.

CHAPTER 7

Nicholas' arrival on the far shores of the Great Sea came sooner than he could have imagined. For so long he had wondered what it would be like to walk where Jesus walked, and now, at age 19, he was finally there.

Finding a boat to get there had been no problem, for his hometown of Patara was one of the main stopovers for ships traveling from Egypt to Rome, carrying people and cargo alike. Booking passage was as simple as showing that you had the money to pay, which Nicholas did.

But now that he had arrived, where would he go first? He wanted to see everything at once, but that was impossible. A tug at his sleeve provided the answer.

"You a Christian?" the small voice asked.

Nicholas looked down to see a boy not more than ten looking up at him. Two other children giggled nearby. To ask this question so directly, when it was dangerous in general to do so, showed that the boy was either a sincere follower of Christ looking for a fellow believer, or it showed that he had ulterior motives in mind. From the giggles of his little friends nearby, a boy and a girl just a bit younger than the one who had spoken, Nicholas knew it was probably the latter.

"You a Christian?" the boy asked again. "I show you holy places?"

Ah, that's it, thought Nicholas. Enough pilgrims had obviously come here over the years that even the youngest inhabitants knew that pilgrims would need a guide once they arrived. Looking over the three children again, Nicholas felt they would suit him just fine. Nicholas had a trusting heart, and while he wasn't naive enough to think that trouble wouldn't find him here, he also trusted that the same God who had led him here would also provide the help he needed once he arrived. Even if these children *were* doing it just for the money, that was all right with Nicholas. Money he had. A map he didn't. He would gladly hire them to be his living maps to the holy places.

"Yes, and yes," Nicholas answered. "Yes, I am indeed a Christian. And if you would like to take me, then yes, I would be very interested to see the holy places. I would love for your friends to come along with us, too. That way, if we meet any trouble, they can defend us all!"

The boy's mouth dropped open and his friends giggled again. It wasn't the answer the boy had expected at all, at least not so fast and not without a great deal of pestering on his part. Pilgrims who arrived were usually much more skeptical when they stepped off their boats, shooing away anyone who approached them—at least until they got their land legs back and their bearings straight. But the boy quickly recovered from his shock and immediately extended his right hand in front of him, palm upraised, with a slight bow of his head. It gave Nicholas the subtle impression as if to say that the boy was at Nicholas' service—and the not-so-subtle impression that the boy was ready for something to be deposited in his open hand. Nicholas, seeing another opportunity to throw the boy off guard, happily obliged.

He gently placed three of his smallest, but

shiniest coins into the boy's upraised palm and said, "My name is Nicholas. And I can see you're a wise man. Now, if you're able to keep your hand open even after I've set these coins in it, you'll be even wiser still. For he who clenches his fist tightly around what he has received will find it hard to receive more. But he who opens his hand freely to heaven—freely giving in the same way that he has freely received—will find that his Father in heaven will usually not hold back in giving him more."

Nicholas motioned with his hand that he intended for the boy to share what he had received with his friends, who had come closer at the appearance of the coins. The boy obviously was the spokesman for all three, but still he faltered for a moment as to what to do. This man was so different from anyone else the boy had ever approached. With others, the boy was always trying, usually without success, to coax even one such coin from their pockets, but here he had been given three in his very first attempt! The fact that the coins weren't given grudgingly, but happily, did indeed throw him off balance. He had never heard such a thought like that of keeping his hands open to give *and* receive. His instinct would have been to instantly clench his fist tightly around the coins, not letting go until he got to the safest place he could find, and only then could he carefully inspect them and let their glimmers shine in his eyes. Yet he stood stock still, with his hand still outstretched and his palm facing upward. Almost against his own self-will, he found himself turning slightly and extending his hand to his friends.

Seizing the moment, the two others each quickly plucked a coin from his hand. Within an instant of realizing that they, too, were about to clench their fists around their newly acquired treasure, they slowly opened their fingers as well, looking up at the newly arrived pilgrim with a sense of bewilderment. They were bewildered not just that he had given them the coins, but that they were still standing there with their palms open, surprising even themselves that they were willing to follow this man's peculiar advice.

The sight of it all made Nicholas burst out in a gracious laugh. He was delighted by their response and he quickly deposited two more of his smallest coins into each of their hands, now tripling their astonishment. It wasn't the amount of the gifts that had astonished them, for they had seen bigger tips from wealthier pilgrims, but it was the generous and cheerful spirit that accompanied the gifts that gave them such a surprise.

The whole incident took place in less than a minute, but it set Nicholas and his new friends into such a state that each of them looked forward to the journey ahead.

"Now, you'd better close your hands again, because a wise man—or woman—" he nodded to the little girl, "also takes care of that which they have been given so that it doesn't get lost or stolen."

Then, turning to walk toward the city, Nicholas said, "How about you let me get some rest tonight, and then, first thing in the morning, you can start showing me those holy places?"

While holy places abounded in this holy land, in the magical moments that had just transpired, it seemed to the three children—and even to Nicholas himself—that they had just stepped foot on their first.

CHAPTER 8

Nicholas woke with the sun the next morning. He had asked the children to meet him at the inn shortly after sunrise. His heart skipped a beat with excitement about the day ahead. Within a few minutes, he heard their knock—and their unmistakable giggles—at the door.

He found out that their names were Dimitri, Samuel and Ruthie. They were, to use the common term, "alumni," children whose parents had left them at birth to fend for themselves. Orphans like these dotted the streets throughout the Roman Empire, byproducts of people who indulged their passions wherever and with whomever they wanted, with little thought for the outcome of their actions.

While Dimitri could have wallowed in self-pity for his situation, he didn't. He realized early on that it didn't help to get frustrated and angry about his circumstances. So he became an entrepreneur.

He began looking for ways he could help people do whatever they needed, especially those things which others couldn't do, or wouldn't do, for themselves. He wasn't often rewarded for his efforts, but when he was, it was all worth it.

He wasn't motivated by religion, for he wasn't religious himself, and he wasn't motivated by greed, for he never did anything that didn't seem right if it were just for the money, as greedy people who only care about money often do. He simply believed that if he did something that other people valued, and if he did it good enough and long enough, then somehow he would make it in life. Some people, like Dimitri, stumble onto godly wisdom without even realizing it.

Samuel and Ruthie, on the other hand, were just along for the ride. Like bees drawn to honey, Samuel and Ruthie were drawn to Dimitri, as often happens when people find someone who is trying to do what's right. Samuel was eight, and like Dimitri, wasn't religious himself, but had chosen his own name when he heard someone tell the story of another little boy named Samuel who, when very young, had been given away by his parents to be raised by a priest. Samuel, the present-day one, loved to hear about all that the long-ago Samuel had done, even though the other one had lived over 1,000 years before. This new Samuel didn't know if the stories about the old Samuel were true, but at the time he chose his name, he didn't particularly care. It was only in the past few months, as he had been traveling to the holy sites with Dimitri, that he had begun to wonder if perhaps the stories really were true.

Now Ruthie, even though she was only seven, was as sharp as a tack. She always remembered people's names and dates, what happened when and who did what to whom. Giggling was her trademark, but little though she was, her mind was eager to learn and she remembered everything she saw and everything she was taught. Questions filled her mind, and naturally spilled right out of her mouth.

Dimitri didn't mind these little tag-alongs, for although it might have been easier for him to do what he did by himself, he also knew of the dangers of the streets and felt compelled to help these two like an older brother might help his younger siblings. And to be completely honest, he didn't have anyone else to call family, so finding these two a few years earlier had filled a part of his heart in a way that he couldn't describe, but somehow made him feel better.

Nicholas took in the sight of all three beaming faces at his door. "Where to first?" asked Dimitri.

"Let's start at the beginning," said Nicholas, "the place where Jesus was born." And with that they began the three-day walk from the coast of Joppa to the hills of Bethlehem.

CHAPTER 9

After two days of walking and sleeping on hillsides, Nicholas and his new friends had just a half day left before they reached Bethlehem. For Nicholas, his excitement was building with every hill they passed, as he was getting closer and closer to the holy place he most wanted to see, the birthplace of Jesus.

"Why do you think He did it?" asked Dimitri. "I mean, why would Jesus want to come here—to earth? If I were already in heaven, I think I'd want to stay there."

Even though Dimitri was supposed to be the guide, he didn't mind asking as many questions as he could, especially when he was guiding someone like Nicholas, which didn't happen very often.

Nicholas didn't mind his asking, either, as Nicholas had done the same thing back home. His parents belonged to a community of be-

lievers that had been started about 250 years
earlier by the Apostle Paul himself when Paul
had visited their neighboring city of Myra on
one of his missionary journeys, telling everyone who would listen about Jesus. Paul had
lived at the same time as Jesus, although Paul
didn't become a believer himself until after Jesus died and rose again from the dead. Paul's
stories were always remarkable.

Nicholas got to hear all of the stories that
Paul had told while he was in Myra, as they
were written down and repeated by so many
others over the years.

As a child, Nicholas thought that anything
that happened 250 years ago sounded like ancient history. But as he started to get a little
older, and now that his parents had passed
away, too, it didn't seem that long ago at all.
The stories that Nicholas heard were the same
stories his father and his grandfather and his
great grandfather, back to six or seven generations, had heard, some for the very first time
from the Apostle Paul in person. Nicholas
loved to hear them over and over, and he
asked many of the same questions that Dimitri was now asking him—like why would Je-

sus leave heaven to come down to earth in person.

"The simple answer is because He loved us," said Nicholas. "But that alone probably doesn't answer the question you're really asking, because God has *always* loved us. The reason Jesus came to earth was, well, because there are some things that need to be done in person."

Nicholas went on to explain the gospel—the good news—to the children of how Jesus came to pay the ultimate price with His life for anything we had ever done wrong, making a way for us to come back to God with a clean heart, plus live with Him in heaven forever.

Throughout the story, the children stared at Nicholas with rapt attention. Although they had been to Bethlehem many times before and had often taken people to the cave that was carved into the hillside where it was said that Jesus was born, they had never pictured it in their minds quite like this before. They had never understood the motivations behind *why* God did what He did. And they had never really considered that the stories they heard about Jesus being God in the flesh were true. How could He be?

Yet hearing Nicholas' explanation made so much sense to them, that they wondered why they had never considered it as true before. In those moments, their hearts and minds were finally opened to at least the *possibility* that it was true. And that open door turned out to be the turning point for each of them in their lives, just as it had been for Nicholas when he first heard the Truth. God really did love them, and God had demonstrated that love for them by coming to the earth to save them from their certain self-destruction.

For Nicholas, when he first heard about the love of the Father for him, the idea was fairly familiar to him because he had already had a good glimpse of what the love of a father looked like from the love of his own father. But to Dimitri, Samuel and Ruthie, who had never had a father, much less one like Nicholas had just described, it was simultaneously one of the most distantly incomprehensible, yet wonderfully alluring descriptions of love they had ever heard.

As they made their way through the hills toward Bethlehem, they began to skip ahead as fast as their hearts were already skipping, knowing that they would soon see again the place where God had, as a Man, first touched earth less than 300 years earlier. They would soon be stepping onto ground that was indeed holy.

CHAPTER 10

It was evening when they finally arrived at their destination. Dimitri led them through the city of Bethlehem to the spot where generations of pilgrims had already come to see the place where Jesus was born: a small cave cut into the hillside where animals could easily have been corralled so they wouldn't wander off.

There were no signs to mark the spot, no monuments or buildings to indicate that you were now standing on the very spot where the God of the universe had arrived as a child. It was still dangerous anywhere in the Roman Empire to tell others you were a Christian, even though the laws against it were only sporadically enforced.

But that didn't stop those who truly followed Christ from continuing to honor the One whom they served as their King. Although Jesus taught that His followers were to still respect their earthly rulers, if forced to choose between worshipping Christ or worshipping Caesar, both the Christians and Caesar knew who the Christians would worship. So the standoff continued.

The only indication that this was indeed a holy site was the well-worn path up the hill that made its way into and out of the cave. Tens of thousands of pilgrims had already made their way to this spot during the past 250 years. It was well known to those who lived in Bethlehem, for it was the same spot that had been shown to pilgrims from one generation to the next, going back to the days of Christ.

As Dimitri led the three others along the path to the cave, Nicholas laughed, a bit to himself, and a bit out loud. The others turned to see what had made him burst out so suddenly. He had even surprised himself! Here he was at the one holy site he most wanted to see, and he was laughing.

Nicholas said, "I was just thinking of the wise men who came to Bethlehem to see Jesus. They probably came up this very hill. How regal they must have looked, riding on their camels and bringing their gifts of gold, frankincense and myrrh. For a moment I pictured myself as one of those kings, riding on a camel myself. Then I stepped in some sheep dung by the side of the road. The smell brought me back in an instant to the reality that I'm hardly royalty at all!"

"Yes," said Ruthie, "but didn't you tell us that the angels spoke to the shepherds first, and that they were the first ones to go and see the baby? So smelling a little like sheep dung may not make you like the kings, but it does make you like those who God brought to the manger *first!*"

"Well said, Ruthie," said Nicholas. "You're absolutely right."

Ruthie smiled at her insight, and then her face produced another thoughtful look. "But maybe we should still bring a gift with us, like the wise men did?" The thought seemed to overtake her, as if she was truly concerned that they had nothing to give to the King. He wasn't there anymore to receive their gifts, of course, but still she had been captivated by the stories about Jesus that Nicholas had been telling them along the road. She thought that she should at least bring Him *some* kind of gift.

"Look!" she said, pointing to a spot on the hill a short distance away. She left the path and within a few minutes had returned with four small, delicate golden flowers, one for each of them. "They look just like gold to me!"

She smiled from ear to ear now, giving each one of them a gift to bring to Jesus. Nicholas smiled as well. *There's always something you can give,* he thought to himself. *Whether it's gold from a mine or gold from a flower, we only bring to God that which is already His anyway, don't we?*

So with their gifts in hand, they reached the entrance to the cave—and stepped inside.

CHAPTER 11

Nothing could have prepared Nicholas for the strong emotion that overtook him as he entered the cave.

On the ground in front of him was a makeshift wooden manger, a feeding trough for animals probably very similar to the one in which Jesus had been laid the night of His birth. It had apparently been placed in the cave as a simple reminder of what had taken place there. But the effect on Nicholas was profound.

One moment he had been laughing at himself and watching Ruthie pick flowers on the hillside and the next moment, upon seeing the manger, he found himself on his knees, weeping uncontrollably at the thought of what had taken place on this very spot.

He thought about everything he had ever heard about Jesus—about how He had healed the sick, walked on water and raised the dead.

He thought about the words Jesus had spoken
—words that echoed with the weight of *authority* as He was the Author of life itself. He
thought about his own parents who had put
their lives on the line to serve this Man called
Jesus, who had died for him just as He had
died for them, giving up their very lives for
those they loved.

The thoughts flooded his mind so fully
that Nicholas couldn't help sobbing with deep,
heartfelt tears. They came from within his
very soul. Somewhere else deep inside him,
Nicholas felt stirred like he had never felt in
his life. It was a sensation that called for some
kind of response, some kind of action. It was
a feeling so different from anything else he
had ever experienced, yet it was unmistakably
clear that there was a step he was now supposed to take, as if a door were opening before him and he knew he was supposed to
walk through it. But how?

As if in answer to his question, Nicholas
remembered the golden flower in his hand.
He knew exactly what he was supposed to do,
and he wanted more than anything to do it.

He took the flower and laid it gently on the
ground in front of the wooden manger. The

golden flower wasn't just a flower anymore. It was a symbol of his very life, offered up now in service to his King.

Nicholas knelt there for several minutes, engulfed in this experience that he knew, even in the midst of it, would affect him for the rest of his life. He was oblivious to anything else that was going on around him. All he knew was that he wanted to serve this King, this Man who was clearly a man in every sense of the word, yet was clearly one and the same with God as well, the very essence of God Himself.

As if slowly waking from a dream, Nicholas began to become aware of his surroundings again. He noticed Dimitri and Samuel on his left and Ruthie on his right, also on their knees. Having watched Nicholas slip down to his knees, they had followed suit. Now they looked alternately, back and forth between him and the manger in front of him.

The waves of emotion that had washed over Nicholas were now washing over them as well. They couldn't help but imagine what he was experiencing, knowing how devoted he was to Jesus and what it had willingly cost Nicholas' parents to follow Him. Each of them, in their own way, began to experience for themselves what such love and devotion must feel like.

Having watched Nicholas place his flower in front of the manger, they found themselves wanting to do the same. If Jesus meant so much to Nicholas, then certainly they wanted to follow Jesus as well. They had never in their entire lives experienced the kind of love that Nicholas had shown them in the past three days. Yet somehow they knew that the love that Nicholas had for them didn't originate with Nicholas alone, but from the God whom Nicholas served. If this was the kind of effect that Jesus had on His followers, then they wanted to follow Jesus, too.

Any doubts that Nicholas had had about his faith prior to that day were all washed away in those timeless moments. Nicholas had become, in the truest sense of the word, a *Believer*.

And from those very first moments of putting his faith and trust fully in Jesus, he was already inspiring others to do the same.

PART 3

CHAPTER 12

Once again, Nicholas was standing on a beach, alone. This time, however, it was on the shores of the Holy Land, looking back across the Great Sea towards his home.

In the months following his visit to Bethlehem, Nicholas, along with his young guide and bodyguards, had searched for every holy place that they could find that related to Jesus. They had retraced Jesus' steps from His boyhood village in Nazareth to the fishing town of Capernaum, where Jesus had spent most of His adult years.

They had waded into the Jordan River where Jesus had been baptized and they swam in the Sea of Galilee where He had walked on the water and calmed the storm.

They had visited the hillside where Jesus had taught about the kingdom of heaven, and they had marveled at the spot where He had multiplied the five loaves of bread and two fish to feed a crowd of over 5,000 people.

While it was in Bethlehem that Nicholas was filled with wonder and awe, it was in Jerusalem where he was filled with mission and purpose. Walking through the streets where Jesus had carried His cross to His own execution, Nicholas felt the weight on his shoulders as if he were carrying a cross as well. Then seeing the hill where Jesus had died, and the empty tomb nearby where Jesus had risen from the dead, Nicholas felt the weight on his shoulders lifting off, as Jesus must have felt when He emerged from the tomb in which He had been sealed.

It was in that moment that Nicholas knew what *his* mission and purpose in life would be: to point others to the One who would lift their burdens off as well. He wanted to show them that they no longer had to carry the burdens of their sin, pain, sickness and need all alone. He wanted to show them that they could cast all their cares on Jesus, knowing that Jesus cared for them. "Come to Me, all you who are weary and burdened," Jesus had said, "and I will give you rest."

The stories Nicholas had heard as a child

were no longer vague and distant images of things that *might* have been. They were stories that had taken on new life for him, stories that were now three dimensional and in living color. It wasn't just the fact that he was seeing these places with his own eyes. Others had done that, and some were even living there in the land themselves, but they had still never felt what Nicholas was feeling. What made the difference for Nicholas was that he was seeing these stories through the eyes of faith, through the eyes of a Believer, as one who now truly believed all that had taken place.

As his adventures of traveling to each of the holy sites came to an end, Nicholas returned to the spot where he had first felt the presence of God so strongly: to Bethlehem. He felt that in order to prepare himself better for his new calling in life, he should spend as much time as he could living and learning in this special land. While exploring the city of Bethlehem and its surroundings, he found another cave nearby, in the city of Beit Jala, that was similar to the cave in which Jesus had been born. He took up residence there in the cave, planning to spend as much time as he could living and learning how to live in this land where His Savior had lived.

Dimitri, Samuel and Ruthie had gained a new sense of mission and purpose for their lives as well. As much as they wanted to stay with Nicholas, they felt even more compelled to continue their important work of bringing more people to see these holy places. It was no longer just a way for them to provide a living for themselves, but they found it to be a holy calling, a calling to help others experience what they had experienced.

It had been four full years now since Nicholas had first arrived on this side of the Sea. During that time, he often saw his young friends as they brought more and more pilgrims to see what they had shown to Nicholas. In those few short years, he watched each of them grow up "in wisdom and stature, and in favor with God and men," just as Jesus had done in His youth in Nazareth.

Nicholas would have been very happy to stay here even longer, but the same Spirit of God that had drawn him to come was now drawing him back home. He knew that he couldn't stay on this mountaintop forever. There were people who needed him, and a life that was waiting for him back home, back in the province of Lycia. What that life held for him, he wasn't sure. With his parents gone, there was little to pull him back home, but it was simply the Spirit of God Himself, propelling him forward on the next leg of his journey.

Making arrangements for a ship home was harder than it was to find a ship to come here, for the calm seas of summer were nearing their end and the first storms of winter were fast approaching. But Nicholas was convinced that this was the time, and he knew that if he waited any longer, he might not make it home again until spring—and the Spirit's pull was too strong for that kind of delay.

So when he heard that a ship was expected to arrive any day now, one of the last of the season to sail through here on its way from Alexandria to Rome, he quickly arranged for passage. The ship was to arrive the next morning, and he knew he couldn't miss it.

He had sent word, through a shopkeeper, to try to find his three best friends to let them know that he would be sailing in the morning. But as the night sky closed in, he had still not heard a word from them.

So he stood there on the beach alone, contemplating all that had taken place and all that had changed in his life since coming to the Holy Land—and all that was about to change as he left it. The thoughts filled him with excitement, anticipation and, to be honest, just a little bit of fear.

CHAPTER 13

Although Nicholas' ship arrived the following morning just as expected, the children didn't.

Later that afternoon, when the time came for him to board and the three still hadn't shown up, Nicholas sadly resigned himself to the possibility that they just might miss each other entirely. He had started walking toward the ship when he felt a familiar tug at his sleeve.

"You a Christian?" came the voice once again, but this time with more depth as about four years were added to his life. It was Dimitri, of course. Nicholas turned on the spot and smiled his broadest smile.

"Am I a Christian? Without a doubt!" he said as he saw all three of them offering smiles to him in return. "And you?" he added, speaking to all three of them at once.

"Without a doubt!" they replied, almost in

unison. It was the way they had spoken about their faith ever since their shared experience in Bethlehem, an experience when their doubts about God had faded away.

As Nicholas tried to take in all three of their faces just one more time, he wondered which was more difficult: to leave this precious land, or to leave these three precious youth whom he had met there. They all knew that God had called them together for a purpose, and they all trusted that God must now be calling them apart for another purpose, too, just as Nicholas had previously felt he was to move to Bethlehem and they were to continue their work taking pilgrims from city to city.

But just because they knew what God's will was, it didn't mean it was always easy to follow it. As Nicholas had often reminded them, tears were one of the strongest signs of love in the world. Without tears at the loss of those things that matter most, it would be hard to tell if those things really mattered at all.

A lack of tears wouldn't be a problem today. Once again, Nicholas asked them all to hold out their right hands in front of them.

As he reached into his pocket to find three of his largest coins to place into each of their outstretched hands, he found he wasn't fast enough. Within an instant, all three children had wrapped their arms completely around Nicholas' neck, his back and his waist, depending on their height. They all held on as tightly as possible, and as long as possible, before one of the ship's crewmen signaled to Nicholas that the time had come.

As Nicholas gave each of them one last squeeze, he secretly slipped a coin into each of their pockets. Throughout their time together, Nicholas' gifts had helped the children immeasurably. But it wasn't Nicholas' presents that blessed them so much as it was his *presence*—his willingness to spend so much time with them. Still, Nicholas wanted to give them a final blessing that they could discover later when he was gone, as he often did his best giving in secret.

Nicholas wasn't sure whether to laugh or to cry at the thought of this final gift to them, so he did a little of both. Under his breath, he also offered a prayer of thanks for each of their lives, then bid them farewell, one by one. The children's hugs were the perfect send-off as he stepped onto the ship and headed for home—not knowing that their hugs and kind words would also help to carry him through the dark days that he was about to face ahead.

CHAPTER 14

The wind whipped up as soon as Nicholas' ship left the shore. The ship's captain had hoped to get a head start on the coming storm, sailing for a few hours along the coast to the harbor in the next city before docking again for the night. It was always a longer trip to go around the edges of the Great Sea, docking in city after city along the way, instead of going directly across to their destination. But going straight across was also more perilous, especially at this time of year. So to beat the approaching winter, and the more quickly approaching storm, they wanted to gain as many hours as they could along the way.

Keeping on schedule, Nicholas found out, was more than just a matter of a captain wanting to make good on his contract with his clients. It was also soon to become a matter of life and death for the families of the crew on board, including the family of the captain. Nicholas found out that a famine had begun to spread across the empire, now affecting the crew's home city back in Rome. The famine had begun in the countryside as rain had been sparse in the outlying areas, but now the shortages in the country were starting to deplete the reserves in Rome as well. Prices were rising and even families who could afford to pay for food were quickly depleting their resources to get it.

The ship's captain was not a foolish man, having sailed on these seas for almost 30 years. But he also knew that the risk of holding back on their voyage at a time like this could mean they would be grounded for the rest of the winter. If that happened, his cargo of grain might perish by spring, as well as his family. So the ship pressed on.

It looked to Nicholas like they had made the right decision to set sail. He, too, felt under pressure to get this voyage underway, although it wasn't family or cargo that motivated him. It was the Spirit of God Himself. He wouldn't have been able to explain it to anyone except to those who had already experienced it. All he knew was that it was *imperative* that they start moving.

He had thought he might spend still more time in the Holy Land, perhaps even his entire life. It felt like home to him from the very beginning, as he had heard so many stories about it when he was growing up. He had little family waiting for him elsewhere, and up to this point, he was content to stay right where he was, except for the Spirit's prompting that it was time to go.

The feeling started as a restlessness at first, a feeling that he was suddenly no longer content to stay where he was. He couldn't trace the feeling to anything particular that was wrong with where he was, just that it was time to go. But where? Where did God want him to go? Did God have another site for him to see? Another part of the country in which he was supposed to live? Perhaps another country altogether that he was supposed to visit?

As the restlessness grew, his heart and his mind began to explore the options in more detail. He had found in the past that the best way to hear from God was to let go of his own will so that he could fully embrace God's will, whatever that may be. While letting go was always hard for him, he knew that God would always lead him in the ways that were best. So, finally letting go of his own will, Nicholas began to see God's will much more clearly in this situation as well. As much as he felt like the Holy Land was his new home, it wasn't really his home. He felt strongly that the time had come for him to return to the region where he had been born, to the province of Lycia on the northern coast of the Sea. There was something, he felt, that God wanted him to do there—something for which he had been specifically equipped and called to do, and was, in fact, the reason that God had chosen for him to grow up there when he was young. Just as Nicholas had felt drawn to come to the Holy Land, he now felt drawn to return home.

To home he was headed, and to home he must go. That inner drive that he felt was as strong—if not stronger—than the drive that now motivated the ship's captain and crew to get their cargo home, safe and sound, to their precious families.

Storm or no storm, they had to get home.

CHAPTER 15

Nicholas' ship never made it to the next harbor along the coast. Instead, the storm they were trying to outrun had outrun them. It caught hold of their ship, pulling it away from the coast within the first few hours at sea. It kept pulling them further and further away from the coast until, three hours later, they found themselves inescapably caught in its torrents.

The crew had already lowered the sails, abandoning their attempts to force the rudder in the opposite direction. They now hoped that by going with the storm rather than against it they would have a better chance of keeping the ship in one piece. But this plan, too, seemed only to drive them into the deepest and most dangerous waters, keeping them near the eye of the storm itself.

After another three hours had passed, the sea sickness that had initially overcome their bodies was no longer a concern, as the fear of death itself was now overtaking all but the most resilient of those on board.

Nicholas, although he had traveled by ship before, was not among those considered to be most resilient. He had never experienced pounding waves like this before. And he wasn't the only one. To a man, as the storm worsened, each began to speak of this as the worst storm they had ever seen.

The next morning, when the storm still hadn't let up, and then again on the next morning and the next, and as the waves were still pounding them, they were all wondering why they had been in such a hurry to set out to beat the storm. Now they just hoped and prayed that God would let them live to see one more day, one more hour. As wave after wave pummeled the ship, Nicholas was simply praying they would make it through even one more wave.

His thoughts and prayers were filled with images of what it must have been like for the Apostle Paul, that follower of Christ who had sailed back and forth across the Great Sea several times in similar ships. It was on Paul's last trip to Rome that he had landed in Myra, only miles from Nicholas' hometown. Then, as Paul continued on from Myra to Rome, he faced the most violent storm he had ever faced at sea, a raging fury that lasted more than fourteen days and ended with his ship being blasted to bits by the waves as it ran aground on a sandbar, just off the coast of the island of Malta.

Nicholas prayed that *their* battle with the wind wouldn't last for fourteen days. He didn't know if they could make it through even one more day. He tried to think if there was anything that Paul had done to help himself and the 276 men who were on his ship with him to stay alive, even though their ship and its cargo were eventually destroyed. But as hard as he tried to think, all he could remember was that an angel had appeared to Paul on the night before they ran aground. The angel told Paul to take heart—that even though the ship would be destroyed, not one of the men aboard would perish. When Paul told the men about this angelic visit, they all took courage, as Paul was convinced that it would happen just as the angel said it would. And it did.

But for Nicholas, no such angel had appeared. No outcome from heaven had been predicted and no guidance had come about what they should or shouldn't do. All he felt was that inner compulsion that he had felt before they departed—that they needed to get home as soon as they could.

Not knowing what else to do, Nicholas recalled a phrase of his father's: "standing orders are good orders." If a soldier wasn't sure what to do next, even if the battle around him seemed to change directions, if the commanding officer hadn't changed the orders, then the soldier was to carry on with the most recent orders given. Standing orders are good orders. It was this piece of wisdom from his father, more than any other thought, that guided Nicholas and gave him the courage to do what he did next.

CHAPTER 16

When the storm seemed to be at its worst, Nicholas' thoughts turned to the children he had just left. His thoughts of them didn't fill him with sadness, but with hope.

He began to take courage from the stories they had all learned about how Jesus had calmed the storm, how Moses had split the Red Sea and how Joshua had made the Jordan River stop flowing. Nicholas and the children had often tried to imagine what it must have been like to be able to exercise control over the elements like that. Nicholas had even, on occasion, tried to do some of these things himself, right along with Dimitri, Samuel and Ruthie. When it rained, they lifted their hands and prayed to try to stop the rain from coming down. But it just kept raining on their heads. When they got to the Sea of Galilee, they tried to walk on top of the water, just like

Jesus did—and even Peter did, if only for a few short moments. But Nicholas and the children assumed they must not have had enough faith or strength or whatever it might have taken for them to do such things.

As another wave crashed over the side of the ship on which Nicholas was now standing, he realized there was a common thread that ran through each of these stories. Maybe it wasn't their faith that was the problem after all, but God's timing. In each instance from the stories he could remember, God didn't allow those miracles on a whim, just for the entertainment of the people who were trying to do them. God allowed them because God had places for them to go, people they needed to see and lives that needed to be spared. There was an urgency in each situation that required the people to accomplish not only what was on *their* heart, but what was on *God's* heart as well.

It seemed that the miracles were provided not because of their attempts to try to reorder God's world, but in God's attempts to try to reorder their worlds. It seemed to Nicholas that it must be a combination of their prayers of faith, plus God's divine will, that caused a spark between heaven and earth, ignited by their two wills working together, that burst into a power that could move mountains.

When Jesus needed to get across the lake, but His disciples had already taken off in the boat, He was able to ignite by faith the process that allowed Him to walk on water, and thereafter calm the storm that threatened to take their lives when He finally did catch up to them.

"Standing orders are good orders," Nicholas recalled, and he believed with all his heart that if God hadn't changed His orders, then somehow they needed to do whatever they could to get to the other side of the Sea. But it wasn't enough for God to will it. God was looking for someone willing, here on earth to will it, too, thereby completing the divine connection and causing the miracle to burst forth. Like Moses when he lifted his staff into the air or Joshua's priests who took the first steps into the Jordan River, God needed someone to agree with Him in faith that what He had willed to happen in heaven should happen here on earth. God had already told Nicholas what needed to happen. Now it was up to Nicholas to complete the divine connection.

"Men!" Nicholas yelled to get the crew's attention. "The God whom I serve, and who Has given each one of us life, wants us to reach our destination even more than we want to reach it. We must agree in faith, here and now, that God not only *can* do it, but that He *wills* us to do it. If you love God, or even if you think you might want to love God, I want you to pray along with me, that we will indeed reach our destination, and that nothing will stand in the way of our journey!"

As soon as Nicholas had spoken these words, the unthinkable happened: not only did the wind *not* stop, but it picked up speed! Nicholas faltered for a moment as if he had made some sort of cosmic mistake, some sort of miscalculation about the way God worked and what God wanted him to do. But then he noticed that even though the wind had picked up speed, it had also shifted directions, ever so slightly, but in such a distinct and noticeable way that God had gotten the attention of every man on board. Now, instead of being pounded by the waves from both sides, they were sailing straight through them, as if a channel had been cut into the waves themselves. The ship was driven along like this, not only for the next several moments, but for the next several hours.

When the speed and direction of the ship continued to hold its steady but impressively fast course, the captain of the ship came to Nicholas. He said he had never seen anything like this in his whole life. It was as if an invisible hand was holding the rudder of the ship, steady and straight, even though the ropes that held the rudder were completely un-manned, as they had been abandoned long ago when the winds first reached gale force.

Nicholas knew, too—even though he was certainly not as well seasoned as the captain— that this was not a normal phenomenon on the seas. He felt something supernatural taking control the moment he first stood up to speak to the men, and he felt it still as they continued on their path straight ahead.

What lay before them he didn't know. But what he did know was that the One who had brought them this far was not going to take His hand off that rudder until *His* mission was accomplished.

CHAPTER 17

The storm that they thought was going to take their lives turned out to be the storm that saved many more. Rather than going the long way around the sea, following the coastline in the process, the storm had driven them straight across it, straight into the most dangerous path that they never would have attempted on their own at that time of year.

When they sighted land early on the morning of the fifth day, they recognized it clearly. It was the city of Myra, just a few miles away from Nicholas' hometown, and the same city where the Apostle Paul had changed ships on his famous journey to Rome.

It was close enough to home that Nicholas knew in his heart that he was about to land in the exact spot where God wanted him to be. God, without a doubt, had spared his life for a purpose, a purpose which would now begin the next chapter of his life.

As they sailed closer to the beach, they could see that the storm that raged at sea had hardly been felt on shore.

The rains that had flooded their ship for the past several days, and that should have been watering the land as well, hadn't made it inland for several months. The drought that the captain and sailors had told him had come to Rome had already been here in Lycia for two and a half years. The cumulative effect was that the crops that were intended to supply their reserves for the coming winter and for next year's seed had already been depleted. If the people of Lycia didn't get grain to eat now, many would never make it through the winter, and still more would die the following spring, as they wouldn't have seed to plant another crop. This ship was one of the last that had made it out of the fertile valleys of Egypt before the winter, and its arrival at this moment in time was like a miracle in the eyes of the people. It was certainly an answer to their prayers.

But that answer wasn't so clear to the captain of the ship. He had been under strict or-

ders from the keeper of the Imperial store-
houses in Rome that not one kernel of grain
could be missing when the ship arrived back
in Rome. The ship had been weighed in Alexandria before it left Egypt and it would be
weighed again in Rome—and the captain
would be held personally responsible for any
discrepancy. The famine had put increasing
pressure on the emperor to bring any kind of
relief to the people. Not only this, but the
families of the captain and crew themselves
were awaiting the arrival of this food. Their
jobs, and the lives of their families, relied on
the safe delivery of every bit of grain aboard.

Yet without the faith and encouragement
of Nicholas, the captain knew that the ship
and its cargo would have been lost at sea,
along with all of their lives.

While it was clear to Nicholas that God
had brought him back to his homeland, he
too wasn't entirely certain what to do about
the grain. While it seemed that giving at least
some of the grain to the people of Myra was
in order, Nicholas still tried to see it from
God's perspective. Was this city, or any other
city throughout the empire, any more in need
of the grain than Rome, which had bought

and paid for it to be delivered? But it also seemed to Nicholas that the ship had been driven specifically to this particular city, in a straight and steady line through the towering waves.

The whole debate of what they were to do next took place within just a matter of minutes of their arrival on shore. And Nicholas and the captain had little time to think through what they were going to do, as the people of the city were already running out to see the ship for themselves, having been amazed at the way God had seemingly brought it to their famished port. They were gathering in larger and larger numbers to welcome the boat, and giving thanks and praise to God at the same time.

Both Nicholas and the captain knew that only God Himself could answer their dilemma. The two of them, along with the rest of the crew, had already agreed the night before—as they were so steadily and swiftly being carried along through the water—that the first thing they would do when they arrived on shore was to go to the nearest church and give thanks to God for His deliverance. Upon seeing where they had landed, Nicholas knew exactly where they could find that church. It was one that his family had visited from time to time as they traveled between these twin cities of Patara and Myra. Telling the people that their first order of duty was to give thanks to God for their safe passage, Nicholas and the captain and his crew headed to the church in Myra.

As they made their way across the city and up into the hills that cradled the church, they had no idea that the priests inside its walls had already been doing battle with a storm of their own.

PART 4

CHAPTER 18

Nicholas' next step in life was about to be determined by a dream. But it wasn't a dream that Nicholas had conceived—it was a dream that God had conceived and had put in the mind of a man, a priest in the city of Myra.

In the weeks leading up to Nicholas' arrival in Myra, a tragedy had befallen the church there. Their aging bishop, the head of their church, had died. The tragedy that had fallen upon the church wasn't the bishop's death, for he had lived a long and fruitful life and had simply succumbed to the effects of old age. The tragedy arose out of the debate that ensued regarding who should take his place as the next bishop.

While it would seem that such things could be resolved amicably, especially within a church, when people's hearts are involved, their loyalties and personal desires can sometimes muddy their thoughts so much that they can't see what God's will is in a particular situation. It can be hard for anyone, even for people of faith, to keep their minds free from preconceived ideas and personal preferences regarding what God may, or may not, want to do at any given time.

This debate was the storm that had been brewing for a week now, and which had reached its apex the night before Nicholas' arrival.

That night one of the priests had a dream that startled him awake. In his dream he saw a man whom he had never seen before who was clearly to take up the responsibilities of their dearly departed bishop. When he woke from his dream, he remembered nothing about what the man looked like, but only remembered his name: Nicholas.

"Nicholas?" asked one of the other priests when he heard his fellow priest's dream. "None of us have ever gone by that name, nor is there anyone in the whole city by that name."

Nicholas was, to be sure, not a popular name at the time. It was only mentioned once in passing in one of Luke's writings about the early church, along with other names which were just as uncommon in those days in Myra like Procorus, Nicanor, Timon and Parmenas. It seemed ridiculous to the other priests that this dream could possibly be from God. But the old priest reminded them, "Even the name of Jesus was given to His father by an angel in a dream."

Perhaps it was this testimony from the gospels, or perhaps it was the unlikelihood that it would ever happen, that the priests all agreed that they would strongly consider the next person who walked through their door who answered to the name of Nicholas. It would certainly help to break the deadlock in which they found themselves.

What a surprise then, when they opened their doors for their morning prayers, when an entire *shipload* of men started to stream into the church!

The priests greeted each of the men at the door as they entered, welcoming them into the church. The last two to enter were the captain and Nicholas, as they had allowed all of the others to enter first. The captain thanked the priests for opening their doors to them for their morning prayers, then turned to Nicholas and said, "And thanks to Nicholas for having this brilliant idea to come here today."

The astonished priests looked at one another in disbelief. Perhaps God had answered their prayers after all.

CHAPTER 19

The captain's concern about what to do with the grain on his ship dissipated when they arrived at the church as fast as the storm had dissipated when they arrived on shore.

Within moments of beginning their morning prayers, he was convinced that it could only have been the mighty hand of God that had held their rudder straight and true. He knew now for sure he wanted to make an offering of the grain to the people who lived there. God spoke to him about both the plan and the amount. It was as if the captain were playing the role of Abraham in the old, old story when Abraham offered a portion of his riches to Melchizedek the priest.

The captain was willing to take his chances with his superiors in Rome rather than take any chances with the God who had delivered them all. He knew that without God's guidance and direction so far on this journey, neither he nor his men nor the ship nor its grain would have ever made it to Rome at all.

When the captain stood up from his prayers, he quickly found Nicholas to share the answer with him as well. Nicholas agreed both to the plan and to the amount. The captain asked, "Do you think it will be enough for all these people?"

Nicholas replied, "Jesus was able to feed 5,000 people with just five loaves of bread and two fish—and what you want to give to this city is much more than what Jesus had to start with!"

"How did He do it?" asked the captain—almost to himself as much as to Nicholas.

"All I know," answered Nicholas, "is that He looked up to heaven, gave thanks and began passing out the food with His disciples. In the end everyone was satisfied and they still had twelve baskets full of food left over!"

"That's exactly what we'll do then, too," said the captain.

And the story would be told for years to come how the captain of the ship looked up to heaven, gave thanks and began passing out the grain with his crew. It was enough to satisfy the people of that city for two whole years and to plant and reap even more in the third year.

As the priests said goodbye to the captain and crew, they asked Nicholas if he would be able to stay behind for a time. The winds of confusion that had whipped up and then sub-sided inside the captain's mind were about to pale in comparison to the storm that was about to break open inside the mind of Nich-olas.

CHAPTER 20

When the priests told Nicholas about their dream and that he just might be the answer to their prayers, Nicholas was dumbfounded and amazed, excited and perplexed. He had often longed to be used by God in a powerful way, and it was unmistakable that God had already brought him straight across the Great Sea to this very spot at this very hour!

But to become a priest, let alone a bishop, would be a decision that would last a lifetime. He had oftentimes considered taking up his earthly father's business. His father had been highly successful at it, and Nicholas felt he could do the same. But even more important to him than doing the work of his father was to have a family like his father.

Nicholas' memories of his parents were so fond that he longed to create more memories of his own with a family of his own. The custom of all the priests Nicholas knew, however, was to abstain from marriage and child-bearing so they could more fully devote themselves to the needs of the community around them.

Nicholas pulled back mentally at the thought of having to give up his desire for a family of his own. It wasn't that having a family was a conscious dream that often filled his thoughts, but it was one of those assumptions in the back of his mind that he took for granted would come at some point in his future.

The shock of having to give up on the idea of a family, even before he had fully considered having one yet, was like a jolt to his system. *Following God's will shouldn't be so difficult,* he thought! But he had learned from his parents that laying down your will for the sake of God's will wasn't always so easy, another lesson they had learned from Jesus.

So just because it was a difficult decision wasn't enough to rule it out. An image also floated through his mind of those three smiling faces he had met when he first landed in the Holy Land, with their heads bowed down and their hands outstretched. Hadn't they seemed like family to him? And weren't there hundreds—even thousands—of children just like them, children who had no family of their own, no one to care for them, no one to look after their needs?

And weren't there countless others in the world—widows and widowers and those who had families in name but not in their actual relationships—who still needed the strength and encouragement and sense of family around them? And weren't there still other families as well, like Nicholas and his parents, who had been happy on their own but found additional happiness when they came together as the family of believers in their city? Giving up on the idea of a family of his own didn't mean he had to give up on the idea of having a family altogether. In fact, it may even be possible that he could have an even larger "family" in this way.

The more Nicholas thought about what he might give up in order to serve God in the church, the more he thought about how God might use this new position in ways that went beyond Nicholas' own thoughts and desires. And if God was indeed in this decision, perhaps it had its own special rewards in the end.

The fury of the storm that swept through

his mind began to abate. In its place, God's peace began to flow over both his mind and his heart. Nicholas recognized this as the peace of God's divine will being clearly revealed to him. It only took another moment for Nicholas to know what his answer would be.

The storms that had once seemed so threatening—whether the storm at sea or the storm in the church or the storms in the minds of both the captain and Nicholas—now turned out to be blessings of God instead. They were blessings that proved to Nicholas once again that no matter what happened, God really could work all things for good for those who loved Him and who were called according to His purpose.

Yes, if the priests would have him, Nicholas would become the next bishop of Myra.

CHAPTER 21

Nicholas didn't suddenly become another man when he became a bishop. He became a bishop because of the man he already was. As he had done before with his father so many years earlier, Nicholas continued to do now, here in the city of Myra and the surrounding towns: walking and praying and asking God where he could be of most help.

It was on one of these prayerful walks that Nicholas met Anna Maria. She was a beautiful girl only eleven years old, but her beauty was disguised to most others by the poverty she wore. Nicholas found her one day trying to sell flowers that she had made out of braided blades of grass. But the beauty of the flowers also seemed to be disguised to everyone but Nicholas, for no one would buy her simple creations.

As Nicholas stepped towards her, she reminded him instantly of little Ruthie, whom he had left behind in the Holy Land, with the golden flowers in her hand on the hillsides of Bethlehem.

When he stopped for a closer look, God spoke to his heart. It seemed to Nicholas that this must have been what Moses felt when he stopped to look at the burning bush in the desert, a moment when his natural curiosity turned into a supernatural encounter with the Living God.

"Your flowers are beautiful," said Nicholas. "May I hold one?"

The young girl handed him one of her creations. As he looked at it, he looked at her. The beauty he saw in both the flower and the girl was stunning. Somehow Nicholas had the ability to see what others could not see, or did not see, as Nicholas always tried to see people and things and life the way God saw them, as if God were looking through his eyes.

"I'd like to buy this one, if I could," he said.

Delighted, she smiled for the first time. She told him the price, and he gave her a coin.

"Tell me," said Nicholas, "what will you do

with the money you make from selling these beautiful flowers?"

What Nicholas heard next broke his heart.

Anna Maria was the youngest of three sisters: Sophia, Cecilia and Anna Maria. Although their father loved them deeply, he had been plunged into despair when his once-successful business had failed, and then his wife passed away shortly thereafter. Lacking the strength and the resources to pick himself up out of the darkness, the situation for his family grew bleaker and bleaker.

Anna Maria's oldest sister, Sophia, had just turned 18, and she turned a number of heads as well. But no one would marry her because her father had no dowry to offer to any potential suitor. And with no dowry, there was little likelihood that she, nor any of the three girls, would ever be married.

The choices facing their father were grim. He knew he must act soon or risk the possibility of Cecilia and Anna Maria never getting married in the future, either. With no way to raise a suitable dowry for her, and being too proud to take charity from others, even if someone had had the funds to offer to him, her father was about to do the unthinkable: he was going to sell his oldest daughter into slavery to help make ends meet.

How their father could think this was the best solution available to him, Nicholas couldn't imagine. But he also knew that desperation often impaired even the best-intentioned men. By sacrificing his oldest daughter in this way, the father reasoned that perhaps he could somehow spare the younger two from a similar fate.

Anna Maria, for her part, had come up with the idea of making and selling flowers as a way to spare her sister from this fate that was to her worse than death. Nicholas held back his tears out of respect for Anna Maria and the noble effort she was making to save her sister.

He also refrained from buying Anna Maria's whole basket of flowers right there on the spot, for Nicholas knew it would take more than a basket full of flowers to save Sophia. It would take a miracle. And as God spoke to his heart that day, Nicholas knew that God just might use him to deliver it.

CHAPTER 22

Without show and without fanfare, Nicholas offered a prayer for Anna Maria, along with his thanks for the flower, and encouraged her to keep doing what she could to help her family—and to keep trusting in God to do what she couldn't.

Nicholas knew he could help this family. He knew he had the resources to make a difference in their lives, for he still had a great deal of his parents' wealth hidden in the cliffs near the coast for occasions such as this. But he also knew that Anna Maria's proud father would never accept charity from any man, even at this bleakest hour.

Her father's humiliation at losing his business, along with his own personal loss, had blinded him to the reality of what was about to happen to his daughter. Nicholas wanted to help, but how? How could he step into the situation without further humiliating Anna

Maria's father, possibly causing him to refuse the very help that Nicholas could extend to him. Nicholas did what he always did when he needed wisdom. He prayed. And before the day was out, he had his answer.

Nicholas put his plan into action—and none too soon! It just so happened that the next day was the day when Sophia's fate would be sealed.

Taking a fair amount of gold coins from his savings, Nicholas placed them into a small bag. It was small enough to fit in one hand, but heavy enough to be sure that it would adequately supply the need.

Hiding under the cover of night, he crossed the city of Myra to the home where Anna Maria, her father and her two older sisters lived.

He could hear them talking inside as he quietly approached the house. Their mood was understandably downcast as they discussed what they thought was their inevitable next step. They asked God to give them the strength to do whatever they needed to do.

For years, Sophia and her sisters had dreamed of the day when they would each meet the man of their dreams. They had even written love songs to these men, trusting that God would bring each of them the perfect man at the perfect time.

Now it seemed like all their songs, all their prayers and all their dreams had been in vain. Sophia wasn't the only one who felt the impact of this new reality, for her two younger sisters knew that the same fate might one day await each of them.

The girls *wanted* to trust God, but no matter how hard they thought about their situation, each of them felt like their dreams were about to be shattered.

At Anna Maria's prompting, they tried to sing their favorite love song one more time, but their sadness simply deepened at the words. It was no longer a song of hope, but a song of despair, and the words now seemed so impossible to them.

It was not just a song, but a prayer, and one of the deepest prayers Nicholas had ever heard uttered by human tongue. His heart went out to each of them, while at the same time it pounded with fear. He had a plan, and he hoped it would work, but he had no way of knowing for sure. He wasn't worried about what might happen to *him* if he were discovered, but he was worried that their father would reject his *gift* if he knew where it had come from. That would certainly seal the girls' doom. As Sophia and Cecilia and Anna Maria said their goodnights—and their father had put out the lights—Nicholas knew that his time had come.

Inching closer to the open window of the room where they had been singing, Nicholas bent down low to his knees. He lobbed the bag of coins into the air and through the window. It arced gracefully above him and seemed to hang in the air for a moment before landing with a soft thud in the center of the room. A few coins bounced loose, clinking faintly on the ground, rolling and then coming to a stop. Nicholas turned quickly and hid in the darkness nearby as the girls and their father awoke at the sound.

They called out to see if anyone was there, but when they heard no answer, they entered the room from both directions. As their father lit the light, Anna Maria was the first to see it —and gasped.

There, in the center of the room, lay a small round bag, shimmering with golden coins at the top. The girls gathered around their father as he carefully picked up the bag and opened it.

It was more than enough gold to provide a suitable dowry for Sophia, with more to spare to take care of the rest of the family for some time to come!

But where could such a gift have come from? The girls were sure it had come from God Himself in answer to their prayers! But their father wanted to know more. Who had God used to deliver it? Certainly no one they knew. He sprinted out of the house, followed by his daughters, to see if he could find any trace of the deliverer, but none could be found.

Returning back inside, and with no one to return the money to, the girls and their father got down on their knees and thanked God for *His* deliverance.

As Nicholas listened in the darkness, he too gave thanks to God, for this was the very thing Nicholas hoped they would do. He knew that the gift truly *was* from God, provided by God and given through Nicholas by God's prompting in answer to their prayers. Nicholas had only given to them what God had given to him in the first place. Nicholas neither wanted nor needed any thanks nor recognition for the gift. God alone deserved their praise.

But by allowing Nicholas to be involved, using Nicholas' own hands and his own inheritance to bless others, Nicholas felt a joy that he could hardly contain. By delivering the gift himself, Nicholas was able to ensure that the gift was properly given. And by giving the gift anonymously, he was able to ensure that the true Giver of the gift was properly credited.

The gift was delivered and God got the credit. Nicholas had achieved both of his goals.

CHAPTER 23

While Nicholas preferred to do his acts of goodwill in secret, there were times when, out of sheer necessity, he had to act in broad daylight. And while it was his secret acts that gained him favor with God, it was his public acts that gained him favor with men.

Many people rightly appreciate a knight in shining armor, but not everyone wants to be rescued from evil—especially those who profit from it.

One such man was a magistrate in Myra, a leader in the city who disliked Nicholas intensely—or anyone who stood in the way of what he wanted.

This particular magistrate was both corrupt and corruptible. He was willing to do anything to get what he wanted, no matter what it cost to others. Although Nicholas had already been at odds with him several times in the past, their conflict escalated to a boiling point when news reached Nicholas that the magistrate had sentenced three men to death—for a crime Nicholas was sure they did not commit. Nicholas couldn't wait this time for the cover of darkness. He knew he needed to act immediately to save these men from death.

Nicholas had been entertaining some generals from Rome that afternoon whose ship had docked in Myra's port the night before. Nicholas had invited the generals to his home to hear news about some changes that had been taking place in Rome. A new emperor was about to take power, they said, and the implications might be serious for Nicholas and his flock of Christ-followers.

It was during their luncheon that Nicholas heard about the unjust sentencing and the impending execution. Immediately he set out for the site where the execution was to take place. The three generals, sensing more trouble might ensue once Nicholas arrived, set out after him.

When Nicholas burst onto the execution site, the condemned men were already on the platform. They were bound and bent over with their heads and necks ready for the executioner's sword.

Without a thought for his own safety, Nicholas leapt onto the platform and tore the sword from the executioner's hands. Although Nicholas was not a fighter himself, Nicholas made his move so unexpectedly that the executioner made little attempt to try to wrestle the sword back out of the bishop's hands.

Nicholas knew these men were as innocent as the magistrate was guilty. He was certain that it must have been the men's good deeds, not their bad ones, that had offended the magistrate. Nicholas untied the ropes of the innocent men in full view of the onlookers, defying both the executioner and the magistrate.

The magistrate came forward to face Nicholas squarely. But as he did so, the three generals who had been having lunch with Nicholas also stepped forward. One took his place on Nicholas' left, another on Nicholas' right and the third stood directly in front of him. Prudently, the magistrate took a step back. Nicholas knew that this was the time to press the magistrate for the truth.

Although the magistrate tried to defend himself, his pleas of fell on deaf ears. No one would believe his lies anymore. He tried to convince the people that it was not *he* who wanted to condemn these innocent men, but two other businessmen in town who had given him a bribe in order to have these men condemned. But by trying to shift the blame to others, the magistrate condemned himself for the greed that was in his heart.

Nicholas declared: "It seems that it was not these two men who have corrupted you, sir, but two others—whose names are Gold and Silver!"

Cut to the quick, the magistrate broke down and made a full confession in front of all the people for this and for all the other wrongs he had done, even for speaking ill of Nicholas, who had done nothing but good for the people. Nicholas set more than three prisoners free that day, as even the magistrate was finally set free from his greed by his honest confession. Seeing the heartfelt change in the magistrate, Nicholas pardoned him, forever winning the magistrate's favor—and the people's favor—from that moment on.

When Nicholas was born, his parents had named him Nicholas, which means in Greek "the people's victor." Through acts like these,

Nicholas became "the people's victor" both in name and in deed.

Nicholas was already becoming an icon—even in his own time.

CHAPTER 24

Within three months of receiving her unexpected dowry from Nicholas, Sophia had received a visit from a suitor—one who "suited her" just fine. He truly was the answer to her prayers, and she was thankfully, happily and finally married.

Two years later, however, Sophia's younger sister Cecilia found herself in dire straights as well. Although Cecilia was ready to be married now, her father's business had not improved, no matter how hard he tried. As the money that Nicholas had given to the family began to run out, their despair began to set in. Pride and sorrow had once again blinded Cecilia's father to the truth, and he felt his only option was to commit Cecilia to a life of slavery, hoping to save his third and final daughter from a similar fate.

While they were confident that God had answered their prayers once, their circumstances had caused them to doubt that He could do it again. A second rescue at this point was more than they could have asked for or imagined.

Nicholas, however, knowing their situation by this time much more intimately, knew that God was prompting him again to intercede. It had been two years since his earlier rescue, but in all that time the family never suspected nor discovered that he was the deliverer of God's gift.

As the time came closer to a decision on what they should do next, Nicholas knew his time to act had come as well. And in order to make it clear that his gift was to be used first and foremost for Cecilia's dowry, and then after that for any other needs the family might have, he waited until the night before she was to be sold into slavery to make his move.

Once again waiting for the cover of darkness, Nicholas approached their house. Cecilia and Anna Maria had already gone to bed early that night, sent there by their father who had told them not to expect any similar miracle to what happened for Sophia. But somewhere in the depths of his despair, their father still had a glimmer of hope in his heart, a wish perhaps, more than anything else, that Someone really was watching out for him and that his prayers just might still be answered. With that hope, he decided to stay awake and stay close to the window, just in case some angel did appear—whether an earthly one or a heavenly one.

Nicholas knew this might happen, and he knew that Cecilia's father might still reject his gift if he found out that Nicholas had given it. But he also hoped that perhaps her father's proud heart had softened a bit and he would accept the gift even if Nicholas was discovered.

Seeing that the house was perfectly quiet, Nicholas knelt down beside the open window. He tossed the second bag of gold into the room.

The bag had barely hit the ground when the girls' father leapt out of the window through which it had come and overtook Nicholas as he tried to flee. You might have thought that Nicholas had *taken* a bag of gold rather than *given* a bag of gold the way the girls' father chased him down!

Fearing that all his efforts had been wasted, Nicholas' heart was eased as the man didn't rebuke Nicholas but thanked him without even looking at who he had caught.

"Please hear me out," he said. "I just want to thank you. You've done so much already for me and my family that I couldn't have expected such a gift again. But your generosity has opened my eyes to the pride in my heart —a pride that almost cost me the lives of two daughters now."

The girls' father had spoken both breathlessly and quickly to be sure that the stranger would hear him before trying to escape again. But when he looked up to see who he was talking to—Nicholas the priest—the shock on their father's face was evident. How could a priest afford to give such an incredible gift?

In answer to this unasked question, Nicholas spoke: "Yes, it was I who delivered this gift to you, but it was God who gave it to me to give to you. It is not from the church and not from the charity of my own hand. It came from my father who earned it fairly by the work of *his* hands. He was a businessman like you. And if he were alive today, he would have wanted to give it to you himself. I'm sure of it. He, of all people, knew how difficult it was to run a business, just as you do. He also loved his family, just as you do, too."

Nicholas paused to let his words sink in, then continued, "But please, for my sake and for God's sake, please know that it was God Himself who has answered your prayers—for He has. I am simply a messenger for Him, a deliverer, a tool in His hands, allowing Him to do through me what I know He wants done. As for me, I prefer to do my giving in secret, not even letting my right hand know what my left hand is doing."

The look on Nicholas' face was so sincere and he conveyed his intentions with such love and devotion for the One whom he served, that the girls' father could not help but to accept Nicholas' gift as if it had truly come from the hand of God Himself.

But as they said their goodbyes, the girls and their father could hardly contain their thankfulness to Nicholas, too, for letting God use him in such a remarkable way.

As much as Nicholas tried to deflect their praise back to God, he also knew he *did* have a role to play in their lives. Although God prompts many to be generous in their hearts, not everyone responds to those promptings as Nicholas did.

Nicholas would wait to see how the family fared over the next few years to see if they would need any help for Anna Maria, too.

But Nicholas never got the chance. The new emperor had finally come into power, and the course of Nicholas' life was about to change again. Even though Nicholas often came to the rescue of others, there were times when, like the Savior he followed, it seemed he was unable to rescue himself.

PART 5

CHAPTER 25

Back when Jesus was born, there was a king who felt so threatened by this little baby boy that he gave orders to kill every boy in Bethlehem and its vicinity who were two years old and under. Three hundred and three years later, another king felt just as threatened by Jesus, as well as his followers.

This new king's name was Diocletian, and he was the emperor of the entire Roman Empire. Even though the Romans had killed Jesus hundreds of years earlier, Diocletian still felt threatened by the Christians who followed Jesus. Diocletian declared himself to be a god and he wanted all the people in his empire to worship him.

Although Christians were among the most law-abiding citizens in the land, they simply couldn't worship Diocletian. He considered this an act of insurrection, an act which must be quenched in the strongest way possible. By the time Diocletian had finally risen to his full power, he ordered that all Bibles be burned, that Christian churches be destroyed and that those who followed Christ be imprisoned, tortured and put to death.

While persecution against Christians had been taking place for many years under Roman rule, none of those persecutions compared to that which took place during the reign of Diocletian. Nicholas, for his part, didn't fear Diocletian, but as always, he feared for those in his church who followed Jesus.

Having such a visible role in the church, Nicholas knew that he would be targeted first, and if he were taken away, he feared for what would happen to those who would be left behind. But Nicholas had already made his decision. He knew that even if he was killed he could trust God that God could still accomplish His purpose on earth whether Nicholas were a part of that or not. It was this foundational faith and trust in God and His purposes that would help Nicholas through the difficult years ahead.

Rather than retreat into hiding from the certain fate that awaited him, Nicholas chose to stand his ground to the end. He vowed to keep the doors to his church wide open for all who wanted to come in. And he kept that vow for as long as he could until one day when those who came in were soldiers—soldiers who had come for him.

CHAPTER 26

Nicholas was ready when the soldiers arrived. He knew that his time for second-guessing his decision to keep the church open was over. Unfortunately, the days for his church were over, too, as the soldiers shut the doors for good when they left.

For all the goodwill that Nicholas had built up with people in his town over the years, even with the local soldiers, these were no local soldiers who came for Nicholas. Diocletian had sent them with demands that his orders be carried out unquestioningly, and that those who didn't carry them out would suffer the same fate as those who were to be punished.

Nicholas was given one last chance to renounce his faith in Christ and worship Diocletian instead, but Nicholas, of course, refused. It wasn't that he *wanted* to defy Roman authority, for Christ Himself taught His followers that it was important to honor those in authority and to honor their laws. But to deny that Jesus was His Lord and Savior would have been like trying to deny that the sun had risen that morning! He simply couldn't do it. How could he deny the existence of the One who had given him life, who had given him faith and who had given him hope in the darkest hours of his life. If the soldiers had to take him away, so be it. To say that a mere man like Diocletian was God, and that Jesus was anything less than God, was unconscionable.

For all his faith, Nicholas was still subject to the same sensations of pain that every human being experiences. His strong faith did not exempt him from the natural fear that others feel when they are threatened with bodily harm. He also feared the idea of imprisonment, having to be isolated from others for so long, especially when he didn't know how long his imprisonment might last—or if he would survive it at all.

Nicholas knew that these fears were healthy, given to him by God, to keep out any danger and to protect him from anything that might possibly harm his body. But right now, as Nicholas was being forcefully taken away, he wished he could suppress those fears.

"God, help me," he called out as the shackles that the soldiers were putting on his wrists cut into them. This was the beginning of a new kind of pilgrimage for Nicholas—a pilgrimage that would last far longer than his years in the Holy Land.

It would be hard to compare these two journeys in terms of their impact on his life, for how could you compare a journey freely taken, where you could come and go as you please and stop the journey at any time, with a journey that was forced upon you against your will, where even venturing out to catch a glimpse of the sun was under someone else's control and not yours?

Yet Nicholas found that he was able to sense the presence of God in a way that equalled, if not surpassed, all that he had experienced in the Holy Land. As he had learned from other believers, sometimes you don't realize that Jesus is all you need until Jesus is all you have.

Over the course of his imprisonment, whenever the door to Nicholas' prison cell opened, he didn't know if the guards were there to set him free or to sentence him to death. He never knew if any given day might be his last. But the byproduct of this uncertainty was that Nicholas received a keen awareness of the brevity of life, as well as a continual awareness of the presence of God.

Nicholas found that by closing his eyes he could sense God's presence in a way he had never sensed it before. This cell wasn't a prison—it was a sanctuary. And all Nicholas wanted to do was to stay in God's presence as long as he could. Soon, Nicholas didn't even have to close his eyes. He simply knew that he was always in the presence of God.

Of course, his time in prison was also filled with the stinging pain of the worst kind of hell on earth. The soldiers were relentless in their attempts to get Nicholas to renounce his faith. The pain they inflicted ranged from prodding him with hot branding irons and squeezing his flesh with hot pincers to whipping him severely, then pouring salt and vinegar in his wounds. As a result, his back was permanently scarred. The unsanitary conditions of the prison caused Nicholas to experience more kinds of sickness than he had ever experienced before. At times he even wondered if death might be better than what he had to endure there.

It was during one of those times, the darkest perhaps, of the five years he had spent so far in prison, that the door to his cell opened. A light streamed in, but as he looked at it closely, it wasn't the light of the sun, for as far as Nicholas could tell in his isolated cell, it was still just the middle of the night.

The light that entered the room was the light of a smile, a smile on the face of Nicholas' young friend, now grown to be a man. It was the light of the smiling face of Dimitri.

CHAPTER 27

Nicholas had seen few faces in his time in prison, and fewer still that gave him any kind of encouragement. To see a smile on someone's face, let alone a face that Nicholas loved so much, was pure joy.

It hadn't been easy for Dimitri to find Nicholas. Dimitri had come to Myra knowing that Nicholas had taken a church there. But it had been years since Dimitri had heard from his friend, a time in which Dimitri himself had been imprisoned. Having only recently been set free, Dimitri made his way across the Great Sea in search of Nicholas. Dimitri had to search hard to find Nicholas, but Dimitri had come too far to give up without seeing his old friend and mentor, the first person who had shown him the love of Christ.

Using the street-smarts that he had acquired as a guide in the Holy Land, Dimitri was able to navigate his way through or around most anyone or anything that stood in his way. Dimitri's tenacity, plus the hand of God's guidance, helped Dimitri to find his friend, and to find this door which he opened that night for this special visit. It was a visit that, to Nicholas, seemed like a visit by an angel from heaven.

After the door closed behind them, and after an extended embrace, Dimitri sat down on the floor next to Nicholas. They sat in silence for several minutes, neither of them having to say a word. In holy moments like these, words were unnecessary.

The darkness in the small cell was so great that they didn't even try to look at one another, but simply sat there side by side. Dimitri's eyes had not yet adjusted to the pitch-blackness enough to see anything anyway, and Nicholas was content to merely know that his friend was right there by him. Nicholas could hear the sound of Dimitri's breath, a sound which increased Nicholas' joy, knowing that his friend was still alive and was right there in the flesh.

Nicholas drew in another deep breath and with it he breathed in a new sense of life. It was a breath of life that his friend couldn't help but bring with him.

CHAPTER 28

"And how are our two young bodyguards doing?" Nicholas asked at last, referring to Samuel and Ruthie. Nicholas had been praying often for all three of them, as he cared for them as if they were his own young brothers and sister.

Dimitri hesitated. He looked at Nicholas but couldn't say a word. He was eager to tell Nicholas everything that had happened in the years that had passed, about how Samuel and Ruthie continued taking people to the holy places, sharing with others the same good news of Jesus that they had discovered in their days with Nicholas.

Like Dimitri, Samuel and Ruthie had to stop guiding pilgrims when the "Great Persecution" came, as it was now being called. All three of them began spending most of their days seeing to the needs of the other believers

in Jerusalem, believers who were facing imprisonment and death, just like Nicholas.
Since they were not in a high profile position
like Nicholas though, the three of them were
able to avoid being caught longer than Nicholas. But eventually, they too were imprisoned,
being repeatedly questioned, threatened and
tortured for their faith.

Samuel and Dimitri were strong enough to
withstand the abuse, but Ruthie was too frail.
One day, after being treated particularly
harshly, she returned to them and collapsed.
Although she had obviously been crying from
the pain in her body, somehow she had also
managed to keep a smile in her heart.

"How can you do it?" asked Samuel. "How
can you possibly still smile, even after all
that?"

Ruthie replied, "I feel like I've been walking and talking with Jesus for so long now that
even death wouldn't really change that. I'll just
keep on walking and talking with Him
forever."

Ruthie smiled again and Dimitri couldn't
help but smile back at her. But her body was
giving out and she knew it. She could sense

that she was just moments away from passing from this life to the next.

"You can't go!" said Samuel. "You've got to stay here with me! There's still too much work to be done!" But Ruthie was slipping away.

"If you die, I'll just pray that God will bring you back to life!" Samuel was desperate now to hang onto her. But Ruthie just smiled again. She had truly found the secret of living life to the fullest, and nothing, not even death, could take that away.

She spoke, quietly now, with just a whisper. "You could pray that God would raise me from the dead, but the truth is, I've already been raised from the dead once. When we met Nicholas, and he introduced us to Jesus, I was raised from the dead and given a whole new life. From then on, I knew that I would live forever."

With that, Ruthie passed through the veil and into the visible presence of God. The smile that adorned her face in life continued to shine on her face in death, and Dimitri knew where she was. She was just continuing to do what she had always done, walking and talking with Jesus, but now face to face.

Nicholas sat in silence as Dimitri told him the story, taking it all in. As much as he thought he would be sad, his heart began to soar instead. None of this was new to him, of course, but hearing about Ruthie's faith brought his own back to life again as well.

You would think a man like Nicholas wouldn't need to be encouraged in his faith. He had brought faith to countless others, and he was a bishop no less. But Nicholas also knew in his heart of hearts that it was people like him who sometimes needed the most encouragement in their faith. Great faith, he knew, did not come to those who have no doubts. Great faith came to those who have had their faith stretched so far that it had to grow, or else it would break completely. By continuing to trust God no matter what, Nicholas found that he was able to fill in any gaps in his faith along the way, helping it to grow even further.

As sad as he was for Ruthie's passing, Nicholas couldn't help but smile from deep down in his heart the same way that Ruthie must have done on the day that she died. He longed for the day when he could see Jesus face to face, just as Ruthie was now seeing

Him. Yet he loved the work that God had given him on earth to do, too.

"We can't lose, can we?" said Nicholas with a reflective smile. "Either we die and get to be with Jesus in heaven, or we live and get to continue His work here on earth. Either way we win, don't we? Either way we win."

"Yes, either way we win," echoed Dimitri. "Either way we win."

For the next several hours, Nicholas and Dimitri shared stories with each other of what God had done in their lives during their time apart. But nothing could have prepared Nicholas for what Dimitri was about to tell him next. For Dimitri, it seems, had met a girl. And not just any girl, but a girl Nicholas knew very well by now. Her name was Anna Maria.

CHAPTER 29

In his journey to find Nicholas, Dimitri looked for anyone who might know of his whereabouts. When he got to Myra, he went first to the church where Nicholas had served as bishop. Not finding him there, Dimitri took to the streets to see if he could find anyone who knew anything about him. And who did he find in the streets, but the very girl—now a woman—that Nicholas had found so many years ago, selling her braided flowers to anyone who would buy them.

She was no longer covered in the cloak of poverty. Both her inner and outer beauty were immediately evident to Dimitri. He was so taken by her that he couldn't help but be drawn into a conversation. And she seemed to be just as taken by him. She couldn't believe that a man of his stature and faith was willing to talk to her. He was, she thought, the kindest and most impressive man she had ever met.

When Dimitri mentioned his mission, searching for the bishop named Nicholas, Anna Maria gasped. How could this man, this stranger from the other side of the Great Sea, know anything about Nicholas? Dimitri shared the story of how they met, and Nicholas had rescued him from his poverty of faith. Anna Maria couldn't help but share what Nicholas had done for her family as well, saving her two older sisters from slavery by throwing a bag of gold through the window for each of them on the eve of their 18th birthdays.

But then, Anna Maria's smile faded. It was now only a few days until her own 18th birthday, but Nicholas had been taken away to prison five years earlier. No one had seen nor heard from him in all those years. She didn't even know where he was. Although her father had had a change of heart, and wouldn't dream of selling Anna Maria into slavery, he still had no dowry to offer any potential suitor. Without a dowry, as Dimitri knew very well, Anna Maria's future was dim. And with Nicholas in prison, there was no chance he would be able to rescue their family a third time. Anna Maria had taken again to selling her flowers in the street, and although they were more impressive than her earlier creations, she could barely earn enough from their sales to help the family with the cost of food from time to time.

Dimitri listened, and like Nicholas before him, he knew within minutes what God was prompting him to do. He could be the answer to Anna Maria's prayers, and with much more than just a dowry. But he also knew that these things take time, so he just treasured these thoughts in his heart, buying a flower from Anna Maria, thanking her for sharing what she knew about Nicholas and continuing on his way, promising to get in touch with her if he ever located their precious friend.

On the eve of Anna Maria's birthday, Dimitri found himself in the very spot where Nicholas had hidden twice before, years earlier, just outside the open window of Anna Maria's home. The conversation inside was subdued, as Anna Maria and her father prayed, knowing that there was no way for Nicholas to appear again. They put out the lights and headed for bed.

Dimitri waited for what seemed to him like hours, knowing that he couldn't dare wake them and risk exposing his plan. For he had saved up enough in his years of working in the Holy Land to easily fill a bag with golden coins suitable for a dowry. But he couldn't just hand them the money, for he had more in mind than just giving them the dowry. He wanted Anna Maria's father to give it back to him someday, as a wedding gift to him! It was a long shot, and he knew he would need more time to be sure she was the one for him. He also felt this was the best way to make it all work out in the end, even if she wasn't the one for him. Something told him, however, that she was. And with that thought in mind, he made his next move.

Carefully and quietly, he reached over the windowsill and let the bag drop quietly down on the floor below. No one heard and no one stirred. Having done his duty to God and to his own heart, he set off again in search of Nicholas. Two weeks later, Dimitri had found Nicholas, and was now sharing with him the story of how he had met the woman of his dreams.

The news couldn't have been any sweeter

to Nicholas' ears. And again his heart lightened and soared, for even though he was locked away from the rest of the world in his prison cell, Nicholas saw the fruit of his prayers—prayers that were answered in the most incredible way imaginable. He could still make a difference in the world, even from here in prison, even when the world tried to shut him down.

Before Dimitri left that night, he embraced Nicholas one more time; then he was gone. He disappeared through the prison door as miraculously as he had entered it.

It would be five more years until Nicholas would see Dimitri again. Diocletian's grip continued to tighten around the Christians' necks. But during all those remaining years in prison, Nicholas felt freer in his heart than he had ever felt before. No man could keep Nicholas from worshipping Jesus, and no man could keep Jesus from doing what He wanted done.

When the day finally came for Nicholas to be set free, the guard who opened Nicholas' door looked in and said, "It's time to go. You're free."

Nicholas simply looked at the guard with a

smile. He had already been free for quite some time.

CHAPTER 30

Thinking Nicholas must not have heard him, the guard spoke again. "I said you're free, you're free to go. You can get up and go home now."

At the word "home," Nicholas stirred. He hadn't seen his home, or his church, or hardly any other soul than Dimitri for ten years. He stood to his feet and his movements began to accelerate as he responded to the guard's words.

"Home?" Nicholas said.

"Yes, home. You can go home now. The emperor has issued a decree that has set all Christians free."

The emperor he was referring to was a new emperor named Constantine. Diocletian's efforts had failed to constrain the Christians. Instead of quenching their spirits, Diocletian had strengthened them. Like Nicholas, those who weren't killed grew stronger in their faith.

And the stronger they grew in their faith, the stronger they grew in their influence, gaining new converts from the citizens around them. Even Diocletian's wife and daughter had converted to Christianity.

Diocletian stepped down from ruling the empire, and Constantine stepped up.

Constantine reversed the persecution of the Christians, issuing the Edict of Milan. This edict showed a new tolerance for people of all religions and resulted in freedom for the Christians. Constantine's mother, Helen, was a devout Christian herself. Even though no one quite knew if Constantine was a Christian, the new tolerance he displayed allowed people to worship whoever they pleased and however they pleased, the way it should have been all along.

As much as Diocletian had changed the Roman world for the worse, Constantine was now changing it for the better. Their reigns were as different as night and day and served as a testament of how one person really can affect the course of history forever—either for good or for evil.

Nicholas was aware, now more than ever, that he had just one life to live. But he was also aware that if he lived it right, one life was all that he would need. He resolved in his heart once more to do his best to make the most of every day, starting again today.

As he was led from his prison cell and returned to the city of Myra, it was no coincidence, he thought, that the first face he saw there was the face of Anna Maria.

He recognized her in an instant. But the ten years in prison, and the wear and tear it had taken on his life, made it hard for her to recognize him as quickly. But as soon as she saw his smile, she too knew in an instant that it was the smile of her dear old friend Nicholas. Of course it was Nicholas! And he was alive, standing right there in front of her!

She couldn't move, she was so shocked. Two children stood beside her, looking up at their mother, and then looking at the man who now held her gaze. Here was the man who had done so much for her and her family. Her joy was uncontainable. With a call over her shoulder, Anna Maria shouted, "Dimitri! Dimitri! Come quickly! It's Nicholas!"

Then she rushed towards Nicholas, giving him an embrace and holding on tight. Dimitri emerged from a shop behind them, took one look at Nicholas and Anna Maria and rushed towards them as well, sweeping his children up with him as he ran.

Now the whole family was embracing Nicholas as if he was a dear brother or father or uncle who had just returned from war. The tears and the smiles on their faces melted together. The man who had saved Anna Maria and her family from a fate worse than death had been spared from death as well! And Dimitri grinned from ear to ear, too, seeing his good friend, and seeing how happy it made Nicholas to see Dimitri and Anna Maria together with their new family.

Nicholas took hold of each of their faces —one at a time—and looked deeply into their eyes. Then he held the children close. The seeds he had planted years ago in the lives of Dimitri and Anna Maria were still bearing fruit, fruit he could now see with his own two eyes. All his efforts had been worth it, and nothing like the smiles on their faces could have made it any clearer to him than that.

Throughout the days and weeks ahead, Nicholas and the other believers who had been set free had many similar reunions throughout Myra. Those days were like one long, ongoing reunion.

Nicholas, as well as the others who had managed to survive the Great Persecution, must have appeared to those around them as Lazarus must have appeared, when Jesus called him to come out of the tomb—a man who had died, but was now alive. And like Lazarus, these Christians were not only alive, but they led many more people to faith in Christ as well, for their faith was now on fire in a whole new way. What Diocletian had meant for harm, God was able to use for good. This new contingent of Christians had emerged with a faith that was stronger than ever before.

Nicholas knew that this new level of faith, like all good gifts from God, had been given to him for a purpose, too. For as big as the tests had been that Nicholas had faced up to now, God was preparing him for the biggest test yet to come.

PART 6

CHAPTER 31

"And you've still never told her, after all these years?" Nicholas asked Dimitri. It had been twelve years since Nicholas had gotten out of prison, and they were talking about the bag of gold that Dimitri had thrown into Anna Maria's open window five years before that.

"She's never asked," said Dimitri. "And even if I told her it was me, she wouldn't believe me. She's convinced *you* did it."

"But how could I, when she knew I was in prison?" It was a conversation they had had before, but Nicholas still found it astounding. Dimitri insisted on keeping his act of giving a secret, just as Nicholas had done whenever possible, too.

"Besides," added Dimitri, "she's right. It really was you who inspired me to give her that gift, as you had already given her family two bags of gold in a similar way. So in a very real sense, it did come from you."

Nicholas had to admit there was some logic in Dimitri's thinking. "But it didn't start with me, either. It was Christ who inspired me."

And to that, Dimitri conceded and said, "And it was Christ who inspired me, too. Believe me, Anna Maria knows that as much as anyone else. Her faith is deeper than ever before. Ever since she met you, she continues to give God credit for all things."

And with that, Nicholas was satisfied, as long as God got the credit in the end. For as Nicholas had taught Dimitri years earlier, there's nothing we have that did not come from God first.

Changing subjects, Nicholas said, "You're sure she won't mind you being away for three months? I can still find someone else to accompany me."

"She's completely and utterly happy for me to go with you," said Dimitri. "She knows how important this is to you, and she knows how much it means to me as well. I wouldn't miss it for the world."

They were discussing their plans to go to the Council of Nicaea that summer. Nicholas had been invited by special request of the emperor, and each bishop was allowed to bring a personal attendant along with him. Nicholas asked Dimitri as soon as he received the invitation.

The Council of Nicaea would be a remarkable event. When Nicholas first opened the letter inviting him to come, he couldn't believe it. So much had changed in the world since he had gotten out of prison twelve years earlier.

Yet there it was, a summons from the Roman emperor to appear before him at Eastertide. The only summons a bishop would have gotten under Emperor Diocletian would have been an invitation to an execution—his own! But under Constantine's leadership, life for Christians had radically changed.

Constantine had not only signed the edict that called for true tolerance to be shown to the Christians, which resulted in setting them free from prison, but he also had started giving them their property back—property which had been taken away under his predecessor. Constantine was even beginning to fund the building and repair of many of the churches that had been destroyed by Diocletian. It was the beginning of a new wave of grace for the

Christians, after such an intense persecution before.

As a further sign of Constantine's new support for the cause of Christianity, he had called for a gathering of over 300 of the leading bishops in the land. This gathering would serve two purposes for Constantine: it would unify the church within the previously fractured empire, and it wouldn't hurt his hopes of bringing unity back to the whole country. As the leader of the people, Constantine asserted that it was his responsibility to provide for their spiritual well-being. As such, he pledged to attend and preside over this historic council himself. It would take place in the city of Nicaea, starting in the spring of that year and continuing for several months into the summer.

When Nicholas received his invitation, he quietly praised God for the changing direction of his world. While the Great Persecution had deepened the faith of many of those who survived it, that same persecution had taken its toll on the ability of many others, severely limiting their ability to teach, preach and reach those around them with the life-changing message of Christ.

Now those barriers had been removed—with the support and approval of the emperor himself. The only barriers that remained were within the hearts and minds of those who would hear the good news, and would have to decide for themselves what they were going to do with it.

As for Nicholas, he had grown in influence and respect in Myra, as well as the region around him. His great wealth was long since gone, for he had given most of it away when he saw the Great Persecution coming, and what remained had been discovered and ransacked while he was in prison. But what he lost in wealth he made up for in influence, for his heart and actions were still bent towards giving—no matter what he had or didn't have to give. After giving so much of himself to the people around him, he was naturally among those who were chosen to attend the upcoming council. It would turn out to become one of the most momentous events in history, not to mention one of the most memorable events in his own life—but not necessarily for a reason he would want to remember.

CHAPTER 32

Although Christians were enjoying a new kind of freedom under Constantine, the future of Christianity was still at risk. The threats no longer came from outside the church, but from within. Factions had begun to rise inside the ranks of the growing church, with intense discussions surrounding various theological points which had very practical implications.

In particular, a very small but vocal group, led by a man named Arius, had started to gain attention as they began to question whether Jesus was actually divine or not.

Was Jesus merely a man? Or was He, in fact, one with God in His very essence? To men like Nicholas and Dimitri, the question was hardly debatable, for they had devoted their entire lives to following Jesus as their Lord. They had risked everything to follow Him in word and deed. He was their Lord,

their Savior, their Light and their Hope. Like
many of the others who would be attending
the council, it was not their robes or outer
garments that bore witness to their faith in
Christ, but the scars and wounds they bore in
their flesh as they suffered for Him. They had
risked their lives under the threat of death for
worshipping Christ as divine, rather than Emperor Diocletian. There was no question in
their minds regarding this issue. But still there
were some who, like Arius, felt this was a
question that was up for debate.

In Arius' zeal to see that people worshipped God alone, Arius could not conceive
that any man, even one as good as Jesus,
could claim to be one with God without blas-
pheming the name of God Himself. In this,
Arius was not unlike those who persecuted Jesus while He was still alive. Even some of
those who were living then and had witnessed
His miracles with their own eyes, and heard
Jesus' words with their own ears, could not
grasp that Jesus could possibly be telling the
truth when He said, "I and the Father are
one." And for this, they brought Jesus to
Herod, and then to Pilate, to have Him crucified.

As a boy, Nicholas had wondered about Jesus' claim, too. But when Nicholas was in Bethlehem, it all finally made perfect sense to him—that God Himself had come down from heaven to earth as a man to take on the sins of the world once and for all as God in the flesh.

Arius, however, was like the Apostle Paul before he met the Jesus on the road to Damascus. Before his life-changing experience, the Apostle Paul wanted to protect what he felt to be the divinity of God by persecuting anyone who said they worshipped Jesus as God. For no man, according to Paul's earlier way of thinking, could possibly consider himself to be one with God.

Like Arius, Paul could not believe the claims of Jesus and His followers. But on the road to Damascus, as Paul was on his way to round up and kill more Christians in his zeal, Paul met the Living Christ in a vision that blinded him physically, but awakened him spiritually to the Truth. In the days that followed, Paul's physical eyes were healed and he repented of his misguided efforts. He was baptized in Jesus' name and began to preach from then on that Jesus was not merely a man, but that Jesus' claims about Himself to be one with the Father were completely true. Paul gave his life in worship and service to Christ, and had to endure, like Nicholas had to endure, imprisonment and an ever-present threat of death for his faith.

Arius was more like the religious leaders of Jesus' day who, in their zeal to defend God, actually crucified the Lord of all creation. Arius felt justified in trying to gather support among the bishops for his position.

Nicholas and Dimitri didn't think Arius' ideas could possibly gather many supporters. Yet they would soon find out that Arius' personal charisma and his excellent oratorial skills might actually hold sway over some of the bishops who had not yet given the idea nor its implications full consideration.

Nicholas and Dimitri, however, like the Apostle Paul, the Apostle John and tens of thousands of others in the time since Jesus lived and died and rose again from the dead, had discovered that Jesus was, thankfully and supernaturally, both fully human and fully divine.

But what would the rest of the bishops conclude? And what would they teach as truth to others for the countless generations to come? This was to become one of the pivotal questions that was to be determined at this meeting in Nicaea. Although Nicholas was interested in this debate, he had no idea that he was about to play a key role in its outcome.

CHAPTER 33

After a grand processional of bishops and priests, a boys' choir and Constantine's opening words, one of the first topics addressed at the council was the one brought forth by Arius—whether or not Jesus Christ was divine.

Arius made his opening arguments with great eloquence and great persuasion in the presence of Constantine and the rest of the assembly. Jesus was, he asserted, perhaps the foremost of all created beings. But to be co-equal with God, one in substance and essence with Him, was impossible—at least according to Arius. No one could be one with God, he said.

Nicholas listened in silence, along with every other bishop in that immense room. Respect for the speaker, especially in the presence of the emperor, took precedence over any type of muttering or disturbance that might accompany other types of gatherings like this, especially on a subject of such intensity. But the longer Arius spoke, the harder it became for Nicholas to sit in silence.

After all, Nicholas' parents had given their lives for the honor of serving Christ their Lord. Nicholas himself had been overwhelmed by the presence of God in Bethlehem, at the very spot where God made His first appearance as Man in the flesh. Dimitri, Samuel and Ruthie had all been similarly affected by that visit to Bethlehem. They had walked up the hill in Jerusalem where the King of kings had been put to death by religious leaders—leaders who, like Arius, doubted Jesus' claims to be one with God.

Nicholas had always realized that Jesus was unlike any other man who had ever lived. And after Jesus died, He had risen from the dead, appeared to the twelve disciples and then appeared to more than 500 others who were living in Jerusalem at the time. What kind of man could do that? Was it just a mass hallucination? Was it just wishful thinking on the part of religious fanatics? But these weren't just fans, they were followers who were willing to give up their lives, too, for their Lord and Savior.

The arguments continued to run through Nicholas' head. Hadn't the prophet Micah foretold, hundreds of years before Jesus was born, that the Messiah would be "from of old, from ancient times"? Hadn't the Apostle John said that Jesus "was with God in the beginning," concluding that Jesus "was God."

Like others had tried to suggest, Arius said that Jesus had never claimed to be God. But Nicholas knew the Scriptures well enough to know that Jesus had said, "I and the Father are one. Anyone who has seen Me has seen the Father... Don't you believe that I am in the Father, and that the Father is in Me?"

Even Jesus' detractors at the time that He was living said that the reason they wanted to stone Jesus was because Jesus claimed to be God. The Scriptures said that these detractors cornered Jesus one day and Jesus said, "I have shown you many great miracles from the Father. For which of these do you stone me?"

They replied, "We are not stoning you for any of these, but for blasphemy, because you, a mere man, claim to be God."

Jesus had certainly claimed to be God, a

claim that got Him into hot water more than once. His claim showed that He was either a madman or a liar—or that He was telling the Truth.

Nicholas' mind flooded with Scriptures like these, as well as with memories of the years he had spent in prison—years he would never get back again—all because he was unwilling to worship Diocletian as a god, but was fully willing to worship Jesus as God. How could Nicholas remain silent and let Arius go on like this? How could anyone else in the room take it, he thought? Nicholas had no idea.

"There was nothing divine about him," Arius said with conviction. "He was just a man, just like any one of us."

Without warning, and without another moment to think about what he was doing, Nicholas stood to his feet. Then his feet, as if they had a mind of their own, began to walk deliberately and intently across the massive hall towards Arius. Arius continued talking until Nicholas finally stood directly in front of him.

Arius stopped. This breach of protocol was unprecedented.

In the silence that followed, Nicholas turned his back towards Arius and pulled down the robes from his own back, revealing the hideous scars he had gotten while in prison. Nicholas said, "I didn't get these for 'just a man.'"

Turning back towards Arius and facing him squarely, Nicholas saw the smug smile return to Arius' face. Arius said, "Well, it looks like you were mistaken." Then Arius started up his speech again as if nothing at all had happened.

That's when Nicholas did the unthinkable. With no other thought than to stop this man from speaking against his Lord and Savior, and in plain site of the emperor and everyone else in attendance, Nicholas clenched his fist. He pulled back his arm and he punched Arius hard in the face.

Arius stumbled and fell back, both from the impact of the blow and from the shock that came with it. Nicholas, too, was stunned —along with everyone else in the room. With the same deliberate and intentional steps which he had taken to walk up to Arius, Nicholas now walked back to his chair and took his seat.

A collective gasp echoed through the hall when Nicholas struck Arius, followed by an eruption of commotion when Nicholas sat back down in his seat. The disruption threatened to throw the entire proceedings into chaos. The vast majority of those in the room looked like they could have jumped to their feet and given Nicholas a standing ovation for this bold act—including, by the look on his face, even the emperor himself! But to others, Arius chief among them, no words nor displays of emotion could express their outrage. Everyone knew what an awful offense Nicholas had just committed. It was, in fact, illegal for anyone to use violence of any kind in the presence of the emperor. The punishment for such an act was to immediately cut off the hand of anyone who struck another person in the presence of the emperor.

Constantine knew the law, of course, but also knew Nicholas. He had once even had a dream about Nicholas in which Nicholas warned Constantine to grant a stay of execution to three men in Constantine's court—a warning which Constantine heeded and acted upon in real life. When Constantine shared that dream with one of his generals, the general recounted to Constantine what Nicholas had done for the three innocent men back in Myra, for the general was one of the three who had seen Nicholas' bravery in person.

Although Nicholas' actions against Arius may have appeared rash, Constantine admired Nicholas' pluck. Known for his quick thinking and fast action, Constantine raised his hand and brought an instant silence to the room as he did so. "This is certainly a surprise to us all," he said. "And while the penalty for an act such in my presence is clear, I would prefer to defer this matter to the leaders of the council instead. These are your proceedings and I will defer to your wisdom to conduct them as you see fit."

Constantine had bought both time and goodwill among the various factions. The council on the whole seemed to agree with Nicholas' position, at least in spirit, even if they could not agree with his rash action. They would want to exact some form of punishment, since not to do so would fail to honor the rule of law. But having been given permission by the emperor himself to do as they saw fit, rather than invoke the standard punishment, they felt the freedom to take another form of action.

After a short deliberation, the leaders of the council agreed and determined that Nicholas should be defrocked immediately from his position as a bishop, banished from taking part in the rest of the proceedings in Nicaea and held under house arrest within the palace complex. There he could await any further decision the council might see fit at the conclusion of their meetings that summer. It was a lenient sentence, in light of the offense.

But for Nicholas, even before he heard what the punishment was going to be, he was already punishing himself more than anyone else ever could for what he had just done. Within less than a minute, he had gone from experiencing one of the highest mountaintops of his life to experiencing one of its deepest valleys.

Here he was attending one of the greatest conclaves in the history of the world, and yet he had just done something he knew he could never take back. The ramifications of his actions would affect him for the rest of his life, he was sure of it, or at least for whatever remained of his life. The sensation he felt could only be understood, perhaps, by those who had experienced it before—the weight, the shame and the agony of a moment of sin that could have crushed him, apart from knowing the forgiveness of Christ.

When Nicholas was defrocked of his title as bishop, it was in front of the entire assembly. He was disrobed of his bishop's garments, then escorted from the room in shackles. But this kind of disgrace was a mere trifle compared to the humiliation he was experiencing on the inside. He was even too numb to cry.

CHAPTER 34

"What have I done?" Nicholas said to Dimitri as the two sat together in a room near the farthest corner of the palace. This room had become Nicholas' make-shift prison cell, as he was to be held under house arrest for the remainder of the proceedings. Dimitri, using his now-extensive skills at gaining access to otherwise unauthorized areas, had once again found a way to visit his friend in prison.

"What have you done?!? What else *could* you have done?" countered Dimitri. "If you hadn't done it, someone else surely would have, or at least should have. You did Arius, and all the rest of us, a favor with that punch. Had he continued with his diatribe, who knows what punishment the Lord Himself might have brought down upon the entire gathering!" Of course, Dimitri knew God could take it, and often does, when people rail against Him and His ways. He is much more long-suffering than any of us could ever be. But still, Dimitri felt Nicholas' actions were truly justified.

Nicholas, however, could hardly see it that way at the moment. It was more likely, he thought, that he had just succeeded in giving Arius the sympathy he needed for his cause to win. Nicholas knew that when people are losing an argument based on logic, they often appeal to pure emotion instead, going straight for the hearts of their listeners, whether or not their cause makes sense. And as much as Arius may have been losing his audience on the grounds of logic, Nicholas felt that his actions may have just tipped the emotional scales in Arius' favor.

The torment of it all beat against Nicholas' mind. Here it was, still just the opening days of the proceedings, and he would have to sit under house arrest for the next two months. How was he going to survive this onslaught of emotions every day during that time?

Nicholas already knew this prison cell was going to be entirely different than the one in which Diocletian had put him for more than a decade. This time, he felt he had put himself in jail. And although this prison was a beautifully appointed room within a palace, to Nicholas' way of thinking, it was much worse than the filthy one in which he had almost died.

In the other cell, he knew he was there because of the misguided actions of others. This gave him a sense that what he had to endure there was part of the natural suffering that Jesus said would come to all who followed Him. But in this cell, he knew he was there because of his own inane actions, actions which he viewed as inexcusable, a viewpoint which he felt many of those in attendance would rightly share.

For decades Nicholas had been known as a man of calm, inner strength and of dignity under control. Then, in one day, he had lost it all—and in front of the emperor no less! How could he ever forgive himself. "How," he asked Dimitri, "could I ever take back what I've just done to the name of the Lord."

Dimitri replied, "Perhaps He doesn't want you to take it back. Maybe it wasn't what you think you did *to* His name that He cares about so much, as what you did *in* His name. You certainly did what I, and the vast majority of those in the room wished they would have done, had they had the courage to do so."

Dimitri's words lingered in the air. As Nicholas contemplated them, a faint smile seemed to appear on his face. Perhaps there was something to be said for his heart in the matter after all. He was sincerely wanting to honor and defend his Lord, not to detract from Him in any way. Peter, he remembered, had a similar passion for defending his Lord. And Nicholas now realized what Peter may have felt when Peter cut off the ear of one of the men who had come to capture Jesus. Jesus told Peter to put away his sword and then Jesus healed the man's ear. Jesus could obviously defend Himself quite well on His own, but Nicholas had to give Peter credit for his passionate defense of his Master.

Nicholas was still unconvinced that he had done the right thing, but he felt in good company with others who had acted on their passions. And Dimitri's words helped him to realize that he was not alone in his thinking, and he took some comfort from the fact that Dimitri hadn't completely forsaken him over the incident. This support from Dimitri acted like a soothing balm to Nicholas' soul, and helped him to get through yet one more of the darkest times of his life.

Although Nicholas was convinced that the damage he had done was irreversible in human terms—and that God was going to have to work time-and-a-half to make anything good come out of this one—Nicholas knew what he had to do. Even in this moment of his deepest humiliation, he knew the best thing he could do was to do what he had always done: to put his complete faith and trust in God. But how? How could he trust that God possibly use this for good?

As if reading Nicholas' mind, Dimitri knew exactly what Nicholas needed to help him put his trust back in God again. Dimitri did what Nicholas had done for him and Samuel and Ruthie so many years ago. Dimitri told him a story.

CHAPTER 35

Dimitri began, "What kind of story would you like to hear today? A good story or a bad story?" It was the way Nicholas had introduced the Bible stories that he told to Dimitri, Samuel and Ruthie during their many adventures in the Holy Land. Nicholas would then begin delighting the children with a story from the Bible about a good character or a bad character, or a good story or a bad story, sometimes which ended the exact opposite way it began.

Nicholas looked up with interest.

"It doesn't matter," Dimitri continued, "because the story I have to tell you today could be either good or bad. You just won't know till the end. But I've learned from a good friend," he said as he winked at Nicholas, "that the best way to enjoy a story is to always trust the storyteller."

Nicholas had told them that he watched

people's reactions whenever he told stories back home.

"When people trust the storyteller," Nicholas had said, "they love the story no matter what happens, because *they* know *the storyteller knows* how the story will end. But when people *don't* trust the storyteller, their emotions go up and down like a boat in a storm, depending on what's happening in the story. The truth is, only the storyteller knows for sure how the story will end. So as long as you trust the storyteller, you can enjoy the whole story from start to finish."

Now it was Dimitri's turn to tell a story to Nicholas. The story he chose to tell was about another man who had been sent to jail, a man by the name of Joseph. Dimitri recounted for Nicholas how Joseph's life appeared to go up and down.

Dimitri started: "Joseph's father loved Joseph and gave him a beautiful, colorful coat. Now that's good, right?"

Nicholas nodded.

"But no, that was bad, for Joseph's brothers saw the coat and were jealous of him and sold him into slavery. Now that's bad, right?"

Nicholas nodded.

"No, that was good, because Joseph was put in charge of the whole house of a very wealthy man. Now that's good, right?"

Nicholas nodded again.

"No, that's bad," said Dimitri, "because the wealthy man's wife tried to seduce him, and when Joseph resisted, she sent him to jail. Now that's bad, right?"

Nicholas stopped nodding either way because he knew where this was going.

"No, that's good," said Dimitri, "because Joseph was put in charge over all the other prisoners. He even helped to interpret their dreams. Now that's good, right?"

Nicholas continued to listen carefully.

"No, that's bad, because after interpreting their dreams, Joseph asked one of the men to help him out of prison when he got out, but the man forgot about Joseph and left him behind. Now that's bad, right?"

Nicholas saw himself as the man who had been left behind in prison.

"No! That's good! Because God had put Joseph in just the right place at just the right time. When the king of Egypt had a dream and he needed someone to interpret it, the man who had been set free suddenly remembered that Joseph was still in jail and told the king about him.

The king summoned Joseph, asked for an interpretation and Joseph gave it to him. The king was so impressed with Joseph that he put Joseph in charge of his whole kingdom. As a result, Joseph was able to use his new position to save hundreds of thousands of lives, including the lives of his own father and even his brothers—the very ones who had sold him into slavery in the first place. And that's very good!"

"So you see," said Dimitri, "just as you've always told us, we never know how the story will turn out until the very end. God knew what He was doing all along! You see...

- at just the right time, Joseph was born and his father loved him,
- so that at just the right time his brothers would mistreat him,
- so that at just the right time the slave traders would come along and buy him,
- so that at just the right time he would be put in charge of a wealthy man's house,

- so that at just the right time he would
  be thrown into jail,
- so that at just the right time he would
  be put in charge of the prisoners,
- so that at just the right time he could
  interpret their dreams,
- so that at just the right time he could
  interpret Pharaoh's dreams,
- so that at just the right time he would
  become second in command over all
  of Egypt,
- so that at just the right time Joseph
  would be in the one place in the world
  that God wanted him to be so that he
  could save the lives of his father and
  brothers and many, many others!

"All along the way, Joseph never gave up
on God. He knew the secret of enjoying the
story while he lived it out: he always trusted
the Storyteller, the One who was writing the
story of his life."

All of Nicholas' fears and doubts faded
away in those moments and he knew *he* could
trust the Storyteller, the One who was writing
the story of his life, too. Nicholas' story
wasn't over yet, and he had to trust that the

God who brought him this far could see him through to the end.

Nicholas looked at Dimitri with a smile of thanks, then closed his eyes. It would be a long two months of waiting for the council's decision. But he knew that if he could trust God in that one moment, and then in the next moment, and then the next, each of those moments would add up to minutes, and minutes would add up to hours. Hours would turn into weeks, then months, then years. He knew that it all began with trusting God in a moment.

With his eyes still closed, Nicholas put his full faith and trust in God again. The peace of God flooded his heart.

Soon, two months had passed by. The council was ready to make their final decisions on many matters, including the decision that had landed Nicholas under house arrest in the first place—and Nicholas was about to find out the results.

CHAPTER 36

"They did it!" It was Dimitri, bursting through the door to Nicholas' room as soon as the palace guard had opened it.

"They did it!" he repeated. "It's done! The council has voted and they've agreed with you! All but two of the 318 bishops have sided with you over Arius!"

Relief swept over Nicholas' whole body. Dimitri could feel it in his body, too, as he watched the news flood over Nicholas' entire being.

"And furthermore," said Dimitri, "the council has decided not to take any further action against you!"

Both pieces of news were the best possible outcome Nicholas could have imagined. Even though Nicholas' action had cost him his position as a bishop, it had not jeopardized the outcome of the proceedings. It was even possible—though he never knew for sure—that his action against Arius had perhaps in some way shaped what took place during those summer months at that historic council.

Within minutes of Dimitri's arrival, another visitor appeared at Nicholas' door. It was Constantine.

The council's decision about what to do with Nicholas was one thing, but Constantine's decision was another. A fresh wave of fear washed over Nicholas as he thought of the possibilities.

"Nicholas," said the emperor, "I wanted to personally thank you for coming here to be my guest in Nicaea. I want to apologize for what you've had to endure these past two months. This wasn't what I had planned for you and I'm sure it wasn't what you had planned, either. But even though you weren't able to attend the rest of the proceedings, I assure you that your presence was felt throughout every meeting. What you did that day in the hall spoke to me about what it means to follow Christ more than anything else I heard in the days that followed. I'd like to hear more from you in the future, if you would be willing to be my guest again. But next time, it won't be in the farthest corner of the palace. Furthermore, I have asked for and received permission from the council to reinstate you to your position as Bishop of Myra. I believe the One who called you to serve Him would want you to continue doing everything you've been doing up to this point. As for me, let me just say that I appreciate what you've done here more than you can possibly know. Thank you for coming, and whenever you're ready, you're free to go home."

Nicholas had been listening to Constantine's words as if he were in a dream. He could hardly believe his ears. But when the emperor said the word "home," Nicholas knew this wasn't a dream, and the word rang like the sweetest bell in Nicholas' ears. Of all the words the emperor had just spoken, none sounded better to him than that final word: home. He wanted nothing more than to get back to the flock he served. It was for them that he had come to this important gathering in the first place, to ensure that the Truths he had taught them would continue to be taught throughout the land.

After more than two months of being separated from them, and the ongoing question of what would become of them and the hundreds of thousands of others like them in the future who would be affected by their decisions here, Nicholas could finally go home. He was free again in more ways than one.

PART 7

CHAPTER 37

Nicholas stood at his favorite spot in the world one last time: by the sea. Eighteen years had passed since he had retuned to Myra from the council in Nicaea. In the days since coming home, he continued to serve the Lord as he had always done: with all his heart, soul, mind and strength.

Nicholas had come to the shore with Dimitri and Anna Maria, who had brought with them one of their grandchildren, a young girl seven years old, named Ruthie.

Ruthie had been running back and forth in the waves, as Dimitri and Anna Maria tried to keep up with her. Nicholas had plenty of time to look out over the sea and as he often did, look out over eternity as well.

Looking back on his life, Nicholas never knew if he really accomplished what he wanted to in life: to make a difference in the world. He had seen glimpses along the way, of course, in the lives of people like Dimitri, Samuel, Ruthie, Sophia, Cecilia and Anna Maria.

He had also learned from people like the ship's captain that when the captain arrived in Rome, his ship miraculously weighed exactly the same as before he had set sail from Alexandria—even after giving the people of Myra several years' worth of grain from it. Reminders like these encouraged Nicholas that God really had been guiding him in his decisions.

He still had questions though. He never quite knew if he had done the right thing at the council in Nicaea. He never quite knew if his later private conversations with Constantine might have impacted the emperor's personal faith in Christ.

He was encouraged, however, to learn that Constantine's mother had also made a pilgrimage to the Holy Land just as Nicholas had done. And after her visit, she persuaded Constantine to build churches over the holy sites she had seen. She had recently completed building a church in Bethlehem over the spot where Jesus was born, as well as a church in

Jerusalem over the spot where Jesus had died and risen from the dead.

Nicholas knew he had had both successes and mistakes in his life. But looking back over it, he couldn't always tell which was which! Those times that he thought were the valleys turned out to be the mountaintops, and the mountaintops turned out to be valleys. But the most important thing, he reminded himself, was that he trusted God in all things, knowing that God could work anything for good for those who loved Him, who were called according to His purpose.

What the future held for the world, Nicholas had no idea. But he knew that he had done what he could with the time that he had. He tried to love God and love others as Jesus had called him to do. And where he had failed along the way, he trusted that Jesus could cover those failures, too, just as Jesus had covered his sins by dying on the cross.

As Nicholas' father had done before him, Nicholas looked out over the sea again, too. Then closing his eyes, he asked God for strength for the next journey he was about to take.

He let the sun warm his face, then he

opened the palms of his hands and let the breeze lift them into the air. He praised God as the warm breeze floated gently through his fingertips.

Little Ruthie returned from splashing in the water, followed closely by Dimitri and Anna Maria. Ruthie looked up at Nicholas, with his eyes closed and his hands raised towards heaven. Reaching out to him, she tugged at his clothes and asked, "Nicholas, have you ever *seen* God?"

Nicholas opened his eyes and looked down at Ruthie, then smiled up at Dimitri and Anna Maria. He looked out at the sunshine and the waves and the miles and miles of shoreline that stretched out in both directions before him. Turning his face back towards Ruthie, Nicholas said, "Yes, Ruthie, I have see God. And the older I get, the more I see Him everywhere I look."

Ruthie smiled, and Nicholas gave her a warm hug. Then just as quickly as she had run up to him, she ran off again to play.

Nicholas exchanged smiles with Dimitri and Anna Maria, then they, too, were off again, chasing Ruthie down the beach.

Nicholas looked one last time at the beautiful sea, then turned and headed towards home.

EPILOGUE

So now you know a little bit more about me—Dimitri Alexander—and my good friend, Nicholas. That was the last time I saw him, until this morning. He had asked if he could spend a few days alone, just him and the Lord that he loved. He said he had one more journey to prepare for. Anna Maria and I guessed, of course, just what he meant.

We knew he was probably getting ready to go home, to his real home, the one that Jesus had said He was going to prepare for each of us who believe in Him.

Nicholas had been looking forward to this trip his whole life. Not that he wanted to shortchange a single moment of the life that God that had given him here on earth, for he knew that this life had a uniquely important purpose as well, or else God would never have created it with such beauty and precision and marvelous mystery.

But as Nicholas' life here on earth wound down, he said he was ready. He was ready to go, and he looked forward to everything that God had in store for him next.

So when Nicholas sent word this morning for Anna Maria and me and a few other friends to come and see him, we knew that the time had come.

As we came into this room, we found him lying on his bed, just as he is right now. He was breathing quietly and he motioned for us to come close. We couldn't hold back our tears, and he didn't try to stop us. He knew how hard it was to say goodbye to those we love. But he also made it easier for us. He smiled one more time and spoke softly, saying the same words that he had spoken when Ruthie had died many years before: "Either way we win," he said. "Either way we win."

"Yes, Nicholas," I said. "Either way we win." Then the room became quiet again. Nicholas closed his eyes and fell asleep for the last time. No one moved. No one said a word.

This man who lay before us slept as if it were just another night in his life. But we knew this was a holy moment. Nicholas had just entered into the presence of the Lord. As

Nicholas had done throughout his life, we were sure he was doing right now in heaven, walking and talking and laughing with Jesus, but now they were face to face.

We could only imagine what Nicholas might be saying to Jesus. But we knew for certain what Jesus was saying to him: "Well done, My good and faithful servant. Well done. Come and share your Master's happiness."

I have no idea how history might remember Nicholas, if it will remember him at all. He was no emperor like Constantine. He was no tyrant like Diocletian. He was no orator like Arius. He was simply a Christian trying to live out his faith, touching one life at a time as best he knew how.

Nicholas may have wondered if his life made any difference. I know my answer, and now that you know his story, I'll let you decide for yourself. In the end, I suppose only God really knows just how many lives were touched by this remarkable man.

But what I do know this: each of us has just one life to live. But if we live it right, as Nicholas did, one life is all we need.

CONCLUSION
by Eric Elder

What Nicholas didn't know, and what no one who knew him could have possibly imagined, was just how far and wide this one life would reach—not only throughout the world, but also throughout the ages.

He was known to his parents as their beloved son, and to those in his city as their beloved bishop. But he has become known to us by another name: Saint Nicholas.

The biblical word for "saint" literally means "believer." The Bible talks about the saints in Ephesus, the saints in Rome, the saints in Philippi and the saints in Jerusalem. Each time the word saints refers to the believers who were in those cities. So Nicholas rightly became known as "Saint Nicholas," or to say it another way, "Nicholas, The Believer." The Latin translation is "Santa Nicholas," and in Dutch "Sinterklaas," from which we get the name "Santa Claus."

His good name and his good deeds have been an inspiration to so many, that the day he passed from this life to the next, on December 6th, 343 A.D., is still celebrated by people throughout the world.

Many legends have been told about Nicholas over the years, some giving him qualities that make him seem larger than life. But the reason that so many legends of any kind grow, including those told about Saint Nicholas, is often because the people about whom they're told were larger than life themselves. They were people who were so good or so well-respected that every good deed becomes attributed to them, as if they had done them themselves.

While not all the stories attributed to Nicholas can be traced to the earliest records of his life, the histories that were recorded closest to the time period in which he lived *do* record many of the stories found in this book. To help you sort through them, here's what we do know:

- Nicholas was born sometime between

260-280 A.D. in the city of Patara, a city you can still visit today in modern-day Turkey, on the northern coast of the Mediterranean Sea.

- Nicholas' parents were devout Christians who died in a plague when Nicholas was young, leaving him with a sizable inheritance.

- Nicholas made a pilgrimage to the Holy Land and lived there for a number of years before returning to his home province of Lycia.

- Nicholas traveled across the Mediterranean Sea in a ship that was caught in a storm. After praying, his ship reached its destination as if someone was miraculously holding the rudder steady. The rudder of a ship is also called a tiller, and sailors on the Mediterranean Sea today still wish each other luck by saying, "May Nicholas hold the tiller!"

- When Nicholas returned from the Holy Land, he took up residence in the city of Myra, about 30 miles from his hometown of Patara. Nicholas became the bishop of Myra and lived there the rest of his life.

- Nicholas secretly gave three gifts of gold on three separate occasions to a man whose daughters were to be sold into slavery because he had no money to offer to potential husbands as a dowry. The family discovered Nicholas was the mysterious donor on one of his attempts, which is why we know the story today. In this version of the story, we've added the twist of having Nicholas deliver the first two gifts, and Dimitri deliver the third, to capture the idea that many gifts were given back then, and are still given today, in the name of Saint Nicholas, who was known for such deeds. The theme of redemption is also so closely associated with this story from Saint Nicholas' life, that if you pass by a pawn shop today, you will often see three golden balls in their logo, representing the three bags of gold that Nicholas gave to spare these girls from their unfortunate fate.

- Nicholas pled for the lives of three innocent men who were unjustly condemned to death by a magistrate in Myra, taking the sword directly from the executioner's hand.

- "Nicholas, Bishop of Myra" is listed on some, but not all, of the historical documents which record those who attended the real Council of Nicaea, which was convened by Emperor Constantine in 325 A.D. One of the council's main decisions addressed the divinity of Christ, resulting in the writing of the Nicene Creed—a creed which is still recited in many churches today. Some historians say that Nicholas' name does not appear on *all* the record books of this council because of his banishment from the proceedings after striking Arius for denying that Christ was divine. Nicholas is, however, listed on at least five of these ancient record books, including the earliest known Greek manuscript of the event.

- The Nicene Creed was adopted at the Council of Nicaea and has become one of the most widely used, brief statements of the Christian faith. The original version reads, in part, as translated from the Greek: *"We believe in one God, the Father Almighty, Maker of all things visible and invisible. And in one Lord Jesus Christ, the Son of God, begotten of the Father, the only-begotten; that is, of the essence of the Father, God of God, Light of Light, very God of very God, begotten, not made, being of one substance with the Father; By whom all things were made both in heaven and on earth; Who for us men, and for our salvation, came down and was incarnate and was made man; He suffered, and the third day He rose again, ascended into heaven; From thence he shall come to judge the quick and the dead..."* Subsequent versions, beginning as early as 381 A.D., have altered and clarified some of the original statements, resulting in a few similar, but not quite identical statements that are now in use.

- Nicholas is recorded as having done much for the people of Myra, including securing grain from a ship traveling from Alexandria to Rome, which saved the people in that region from a famine.

• Constantine's mother, Helen, did visit
  the Holy Land and encouraged Constantine to build churches over the
  sites that she felt were most important
  to the Christian faith. The churches
  were built on the locations she had
  been shown by local believers where
  Jesus was born, and where Jesus died
  and rose again. Those churches, The
  Church of the Nativity in Bethlehem
  and the Church of the Holy Sepulchre
  in Jerusalem, have been destroyed and
  rebuilt many times over the years, but
  still in the same locations that Constantine's mother, and likely Nicholas
  himself, had seen.

• The date of Nicholas' death has been
  established as December 6th, 343 A.D.,
  and you can still visit his tomb in the
  modern city of Demre, Turkey,
  formerly known as Myra, in the
  province of Lycia. Nicholas' bones
  were removed from the tomb in 1087
  A.D. by men from Italy who feared
  that they might be destroyed or stolen,
  as the country was being invaded by
  others. The bones of Saint Nicholas

were taken to the city of Bari, Italy, where they are still entombed today.

Of the many other stories told about or attributed to Nicholas, it's hard to know with certainty which ones actually took place and which were simply attributed to him because of his already good and popular name. For instance, in the 12th century, stories began to surface of how Nicholas had brought three children back to life who had been brutally murdered. Even though the first recorded accounts of this story didn't appear until more than 800 years after Nicholas' death, this story is one of the most frequently associated with Saint Nicholas in religious artwork, featuring three young children being raised to life and standing next to Nicholas. We have included the essence of this story in this novel in the form of the three orphans who Nicholas met in the Holy Land and whom he helped to bring back to life—at least spiritually.

While all of these additional stories can't be attributed to Nicholas with certainty, we can say that his life and his memory had such a profound effect throughout history that more churches throughout the world now bear the

name of "Saint Nicholas" than any other figure, outside of the original disciples themselves.

Some people wonder if they can believe in
Saint Nicholas or not. Nicholas probably
wouldn't care so much if you believed in *him*
or not, but that you believed in the One in
whom He believed, *Jesus Christ.*

A popular image today shows Saint Nicholas bowing down, his hat at his side, kneeling
in front of baby Jesus in the manger. Although that scene could never have taken
place in real life, for Saint Nicholas was born
almost 300 years *after* the birth of Christ, the
heart of that scene couldn't be more accurate.
Nicholas *was* a true believer in Jesus and he
did worship, adore and live his life in service
to the Christ.

Saint Nicholas would have never wanted
his story to *replace* the story of Jesus in the
manger, but he would have loved to have his
story *point* to Jesus in the manger. And that's
why this book was written.

While the stories told here were selected
from the many that have been told about
Saint Nicholas over the years, these were told
so that you might believe—not just in Nich-

olas, but in Jesus Christ, his Savior. These stories were written down for the same reason the Apostle John wrote down the stories he recorded about Jesus in the Bible. John said he wrote his stories:

"...that you may believe that Jesus is the Christ, the Son of God, and that by believing you may have life in His name" (John 20:31).

Nicholas would want the same for you. He would want you to become what he was: a Believer.

If you've never done so, put your faith in Jesus Christ today, asking Him to forgive you of your sins and giving you the assurance that you will live with Him forever.

If you've already put your faith in Christ, let this story remind you just how precious your faith really is. Renew your commitment today to serve Christ as Nicholas served Him: with all of your heart, soul, mind and strength. God really will work all things together for good. As the Bible says:

"And we know that in all things God works for

the good of those who love Him, who have been called according to His purpose" (Romans 8:28).

Thanks for reading this special book about this special man, and I pray that your Christmas may be truly merry and bright. As Clement Moore said in his now famous poem, *A Visit From St. Nicholas:*

"Happy Christmas to all, and to all a good night!"

Eric Elder

ACKNOWLEDGEMENTS

Special thanks to Joe Wheeler and Jim Rosenthal whose book, *St. Nicholas: A Closer Look at Christmas,* provided much of the background material for this novella. Their research and documentation of the life of St. Nicholas, and the historical context in which he lived, was the most informative, authoritative and inspirational we found on the subject. Thank you, Joe and Jim, for helping to keep the spirit of St. Nicholas alive!

About The Authors

Eric & Lana Elder have written numerous Christmas stories that have captivated and inspired thousands as part of an annual Christmas production known as *The Bethlehem Walk.*

St. Nicholas: The Believer marks the debut of their first full-length Christmas story. Eric & Lana have also collaborated on several other inspirational books including:

Two Weeks With God
What God Says About Sex
Exodus: Lessons In Freedom
Jesus: Lessons In Love
Acts: Lessons In Faith
Nehemiah: Lessons In Rebuilding
Ephesians: Lessons In Grace
Israel: Lessons From The Holy Land
Israel For Kids: Lessons From The Holy Land
The Top 20 Passages In The Bible
Romans: Lessons In Renewing Your Mind
and *Making The Most Of The Darkness*

To order or learn more, please visit:
www.InspiringBooks.com